I0417867

WHERE THE DRAGONS GO

C.W. SIMS

For my mom.

Thank you for never giving up on me.

ONE HUNDRED SIXTY-FIVE DAYS

LOOKING AT THINGS is weird, ever notice that? Take passenger seat windows. You can look straight through them if you want, but if you pay attention you can see your reflection too. And it's an odd reflection. Kind of like a ghost. The world rolls by at whatever miles per hour and then there's you, the transparent version, floating on the other side. What I don't get is why. After all, it's a window not a mirror. Fortunately, I know exactly who has the answer.

iPhone. Wikipedia. Done.

Okay, so apparently "light" is made of these tiny things called "photons"—as in "Fire photon torpedoes!"—and they all came from the Sun. They're bouncing all over the place and plants soak them up, and we eat the plants and keep on truckin'. And that's it. Life in a nutshell. Thank you, Internet. Plants, animals, toaster ovens—all powered by particles from the Sun. It's like there's this giant battery a million miles away—er, wait a sec—92 million and 960,000 miles away.

But back to the window. The photons bounce off the glass, then off a bunch of cells in my eyeball. Then my brain tells me there are things like windows and colors in the world, and that Chad Atkins in my first period English class looks cute when his ears go red. And when I think about things like that, my brain's using photons converted from a spinach leaf I ate a few hours ago. Although, let's be honest. It was a bag of Cheetos.

Pretty cool though, right? Clearly worthy of more investigation. I buried my nose in my phone, but my mom wasn't having it. She immediately asked what I was so frantically reading about, yet when it became clear I wasn't going to answer, she said, "Honey, is it... do you have more questions?"

I glanced up at her. The photons bouncing off her face made her look pale, even paler than me. "No, I'm okay," I said.

And so she kept driving the Blue Beast—an absurd 1970s muscle car, officially called a GTO. (She has this love affair with classic cars, so instead of saving the world with a Prius, she drives me around in a Batmobile.) I'd wanted to drive it myself, being the proud owner of a learner's permit and all, but she didn't think it was a good idea. "Another time," she told me.

I said, "What if there isn't another time?" and she started crying. Not *sobbing*, mind you, but that quiet, single tear on the cheek type of crying that she's been doing a lot these days.

Besides, it was only a short drive home. I didn't see the big deal. I felt fine; better than she looked at least—bags under her eyes the size of potato sacks. So I contented myself to the window and photons. It was like a game. I could look at me or I could look at the world, but both at the same time were tough. Plus, there was the third option. I could think real hard about things and not see anything at all. Sometimes that's the best move. Did you know you can go *anywhere* inside your brain? Especially if you have a smartphone. So let's say I've never been to Barcelona, which I haven't. All I need are a few pictures.

Search. Barcelona. Done.

Now I'm walking down a smoky Spanish street on a balmy summer's night and there are lights and parties and music and a cute guy on a Vespa pulls up and tells me my glasses are sexy, and at first I think that's kind of lame, but then I jump on the back anyway and we ride off to a moonlit beach and start dancing and it's the best night of my life.

And that's just *Barcelona*. That's nothing. That's for amateurs. I'm talking about high-speed getaways on the Firefly *Serenity* and debutante balls on the Klingon homeworld of Qo'noS. Can you imagine what one of *those* would look like?

Anyway. I'm getting sidetracked. There was a point to all this. And here it is:

The drive back to my family's domicile—a faux Spanish villa made from Play-Doh—in the ever-sunny landscape of Almaden Valley, California, wasn't a happy one. My mom was sad, and I was doing my best to think real hard about things—all the things except the one thing I most definitely did *not* want to think about.

And right as I was not thinking about that thing, I saw it. A giant, winged shadow whooshed over the Blue Beast. I shot forward to catch a glimpse, but it was too hard to see. The Sun's rays—*countless photons!*—were blasting down from above.

I was still glued to the windshield when I said, "Mom?"

"Can you see it?" she asked, peering up through the glass. "I hope it's not an emergency."

"I think you better step on it," I said.

Technically I wasn't looking at her, but I knew she was making her incredibly intense "worry face" at that precise moment. I'd seen it oh so many times, and when I heard her, I could tell she was nearly hyperventilating.

"Chloe, oh my God. Should I turn around?"

I was way too weirded out to know what to say so I just blinked for a moment before finally saying, "Uh... no. I'm fine. But I think you should really, definitely go faster."

"*Why?*"

I squinted up through the window another moment. "Well, I'm no expert,"—although I kind of was—"but I think I'm looking at a... *dragon?*"

I felt stupid just saying it. I mean, seriously. A dragon? Like an actual, medieval-style dragon? I needed to get my brain examined.

"Chloe, that's not funny!" she screeched. "I thought... God, you had me scared to death!"

I wasn't trying to be funny, but I clamped my mouth shut anyway. Mom didn't yell at me too often, and I knew better than to push her. But honestly, what did I expect? Was she going to say, "Oh really? A dragon?" and then take another look? No. She was a mom. An adult. She lived in the real world. You can't talk to people about dragons in the real world. They'll never, ever believe you.

ONE HUNDRED SIXTY-FOUR DAYS

NO MATTER. My friends were coming over tonight for our weekly, "Friday Night? Game Night!" (Although technically it was Thursday.) I could test my sanity on them. Who better to believe a dragon sighting than three people who still took the game of Dungeons & Dragons incredibly seriously? Sid, Thu and Joshua, that's who.

Mom kept asking if I still wanted them to come over, but I assured her I was fine. No way was I about to ruin one of the best campaigns our group had been on in months.

Plus, I wasn't the Dungeon Master this time so I could finally play my supremely awesome Hafling warrior character, Betty the Bold. Ever since sixth grade when we started playing D&D, she's been my answer to the dread question, "what do you want to be when you grow up?" Although recently I've begun to temper that answer with, "Expert in Pirate Affairs and Professional Treasure Hunter." Imagine if that was on your business card and *wasn't* a joke. Heck of a lot cooler than "tax attorney," that's for sure.

Anyway, Sid was the first to ring the bell. He'd been my best friend for as long as I could remember, but I never *like* liked him. There were several reasons for this, but the primary one—and I know how awful this sounds—was that he was very, very *not* cute. Kinda mean, right? Let's just say he wasn't my type, and I wasn't his. I liked guys who were tall. He was short. I liked abs. He had a potbelly. He did have a great smile though. It was one of those giant ones that literally lights up a room. He was even approached for a toothpaste commercial once, but the rest of his face disqualified him. It was a crushing blow.

Still, he embraced his looks—modeling career or no. In my eyes, that made him a heck of a lot cooler than most kids our age. Or at least, *his* age. He was sixteen with a full-fledged driver's license and a car. I, on the other hand, was still fifteen because I skipped second grade for some silly and unknown reason.

When Mom answered the door, Sid gasped and said what he always says whenever he sees her, which is: "Good God, you're as stunning as ever!" He then thundered into the house carrying a sack full of snacks not waiting for her awkward response. I glided down the stairs and met him in the kitchen, telling him for the thousandth time to stop flirting with my mom.

"She's just so hot," he answered, smiling through a mouthful of Cheetos. "Seriously, does she ever ask about me?"

I punched him on the shoulder out of habit. "God, you're gross."

"But classy," he said, cracking a Mountain Dew.

I should briefly mention that somewhere in gaming history, Mountain Dew and Cheetos became the official snack food of Dungeon's & Dragons. As a player you could either a.) Think you were cool by eating something different, or b.) Think you were cool by embracing the cliché. We chose the latter.

Joshua arrived next. And yes, he insisted he be called Joshua instead of Josh. We didn't call him either. We called him Dawson's Creek, due to his alarming resemblance to the Pacey character. (Who incidentally was played by an actor named *Joshua* Jackson.) One night, Sid and I had been watching old re-runs and noticed the similarity at the exact same time. We promptly ditched the show and spent the rest of the evening making flyers with a side-by-side comparison. No one has ever used Joshua's real name since. *However,* his nickname also implied he was the best looking of our group, which he definitely was. For this reason, I tended to describe my gaming circle as 3.5. He was the point five.

It wasn't that I didn't like him or anything. He was cool and funny and sorta weird—a perfect trifecta of likability. It was just that he was the only member of our D&D group who lived within the paradise of popularity at Stafford High, so he seldom risked being seen with us at school. We all thought this was a little mean, so we made up for it by teasing him relentlessly.

Thu Pham was next. Her arrival completed the group. She and I had been friends since my fourth birthday party—you know, one of those awesome things where you don't have any friends yet so your parents invite a bunch of kids you don't know and everyone awkwardly stares at each other? That's where we met. We started playing this weird headbutting game that we thought was amazing but no one else wanted to join. We finished bruised, but friends.

Since then, we'd grown up to look like identical twins, except one was Asian (Thu) and one was pasty (me). We were both short, super skinny, dark hair (though mine was horrendously curly), and adorned with giant, thick-rimmed glasses that marked us as nerds no matter what we did. We seriously could've gone into the city and gotten sleeve tattoos and nose piercings, and everyone still would've copied our homework.

Once we were all in the kitchen, Sid banged his pencil on the table like a gavel. "A quorum is present," he announced, ushering everyone to sit down. "I say we begin this session by voting on a very important matter."

Dawson's Creek glared at him. "If you say what I think you're going to—"

"The matter before the table," Sid said, "is whether Dawson's Creek should come clean and admit that he totally sucks."

"Here, here." I nodded happily, giving my soda can a couple taps on the table. Thu giggled and did the same.

Dawson's Creek was annoyed. "Do we have to do this every game?"

"Yes," Sid said. "Until you accept yourself for who you are."

"Fine! I'll hang out with you guys more at school, okay? I'm sorry. I'll stop being an asshole. Happy? Can we move on now?"

I threw a Cheeto at him. "*More?*" I snorted.

"What?"

"You said 'more,' as if you hang out with us at school already. Need I remind you of the Yearbook Signing Incident?"

"That was an accident!"

Frowning, I mimed opening a yearbook and did my best impression of a guy voice. "Sup Nicole. You're cool. Keep in Touch. Joshua Travers." I looked up at him. "You are aware my name is Chloe, not Nicole, right?"

Sid shook his head miserably. "That was a new low, Pacey. I mean, what would Joey Potter think?"

"First of all," Dawson's Creek said, "it was an honest mistake. I was thinking about this other girl Nicole and—"

"Forgot my name?"

"No! That's not what happened. I've explained this a thousand times. I was just—"

Thu suddenly raised her hand. "I have a new motion before the council," she said. "I say we vote on if we even *want* Dawson's Creek to hang out with us at school."

Sid laughed, tapping his pencil in agreement. "All in favor of shunning Dawson's Creek next year?"

Three hands shot up.

"Looks like the ayes have it," Sid said. "And now that that's decided, on to the Chamber of Horrors. If I remember correctly, you poor saps were still stuck on finding the Lost Key. Anyone had any bright ideas since last time? Dawson's Creek? You first."

And so Dungeons & Dragons commenced. Although to be fair, like most rounds of D&D, our gameplay consisted of about twenty percent game, eighty percent trash talk—most of which focused on Dawson's Creek. Poor guy. He might have been cool at school, but with us he was like a picture on a dartboard.

We played until ten. As always, it went by in a flash. It was a great distraction from earlier, and somewhere around the midway point I decided against telling them about my dragon sighting. It never felt like the right moment, so I did what Mom advised before they came over. I kept it to myself. But I knew that could only last for so long. Eventually I'd have to tell *somebody*. It was way too big to keep secret forever.

ONE HUNDRED
SIXTY-THREE DAYS

EVERY MORNING, I got jarred awake by the ferocious war cry of Chewbacca. There were two people to blame for this: 1.) Myself. For it was I who had begged for the *Millennium Falcon* alarm clock when I was seven. 2.) My mother. For it was she who had decreed that I set it for 7:00 a.m. every single day for the rest of my life.

Was it a holiday? 7:00 a.m.

Was it a Saturday? 7:00 a.m.

Did a spaceship land in the backyard and I was up all night negotiating a peace treaty with an alien race? 7:00 a.m.

Now you might ask, "Chloe, why don't you just get rid of the thing?" To which I would reply, "Because it's the *Millennium Falcon*, dummy! You know how much this thing is worth?!"

So there you have it. Every single day began with the sound of an accordion being stuffed into a garbage disposal.

I silenced Chewbacca with a quick slap on the *Falcon's* circular sensor dish (you know *exactly* which one I'm talking about) and fumbled out of bed. I went downstairs in my pajamas—also *Star Wars*-themed—expecting to see the usual Cartwright Family Breakfast Routine.

My nerdy, albeit cool, computer programmer dad would be breezing through the kitchen any second because he was super late for work. My beautiful personal trainer mother would be wearing her gym clothes and frantically getting my brother Henry ready for daycare. Our dog, Woz, would be passed out from exhaustion after Mom's morning run. (Poor little guy was a Pug; he wasn't designed to keep up with Wonder Woman.)

Instead, I walked in to find Mom and Dad sitting peacefully at the kitchen table reading their tablets, the smell of fresh gluten-free chickpea pancakes (it's a long story) wafted through the air, and Henry was sitting regally in his high chair, unusually calm and studying a blueberry. Even Woz was upright, tail wagging, and ready for action.

I announced my presence. "Um…?"

They all looked up in unison. "Morning!" Dad beamed, raising his coffee in salute. The mug read: *My Code is Guaranteed 100% Mistrake Free.* It was no secret which parent I inherited my dorkiness from. "We thought we'd all take the day off," he said.

"And I made your favorite," Mom announced with a smile. "Pancakes!"

Favorite was a strong word. It was my *favorite* in relative terms. Any meal prepared by my mom was destined to contain some cruel combination of flax seed, chickpeas, kale or butternut squash.

"You guys are acting weird. What's going on?" I said.

"What do you mean?" Dad asked. "Come have a seat. We didn't want to start without you. There's yoke-less eggs."

Cautiously—these people had clearly kidnapped my family and could have set booby traps—I pulled out my chair and poured some orange juice. Henry eyed me with equal suspicion and then blew a raspberry.

"So," Mom said cheerily, passing me the pancakes. "Today's your last Friday of summer break. Anything you want to do today?"

I wrinkled my nose. My last "Friday?" That was kinda weird. I still had Saturday, Sunday, Monday and Tuesday before school started but... okay.

"Um. I don't know. Go skydiving?"

For a split second—and I'm sure she didn't think I noticed—she shifted uneasily. "Well," she said. "I was thinking more like something the whole family could do. How about the zoo?"

"The zoo?" I asked through a mouthful of eggs. "I'm fifteen."

Dad scoffed. "Oh, Chloe. If there's one thing I've learned after forty years of life, it's that you're never too old for the zoo. Take you mom for example. She's getting pretty old these days and she can't wait to go."

She glared at him. "I'm only a year older than you, *sweetie*. Stop using me as your example for an old person."

He held up a finger. "Fifteen months and six days. So for three months of every year you're *two* years older than me."

"And I can still beat you up," she said. "Remember that."

He grinned. "Is it wrong that I find that attractive?"

I grimaced as the increasingly disturbing conversation continued to unfold, but I couldn't help but think: *Are they bantering?*

There was no way. They'd barely had a full conversation in, like, a year. They were always too busy. And as far as I could tell, the only words that were ever spoken between them fell into one of two categories:

1.) THINGS TO DO WITH HENRY — Have you fed him yet? *Yes.* Has he slept? *No.* Does he need to be changed? *I'll check.*

2.) HOUSEHOLD STUFF — Did you remember to pick up XYZ at the grocery? *No. Crap.* Have you fixed the ABC yet? *Yes.* Have you noticed that leak in the thingamajig? *I'll get to it.*

But *banter?* No. These people definitely were not my parents. Aliens, perhaps? Shapeshifters?

"So Chloe." Dad brought the focus back to me. "Monkeys? Giraffes? Baby Koalas?" He crossed his fingers. "Please say yes, please say yes, please say yes…"

He just *had* to mention the monkeys, didn't he? My weakness.

"Fine," I relented, jutting my chin a little. "But only because Henry will like it."

So that settled it. An hour later we were at the zoo. I waged a protest of determined indifference by keeping my nose glued to my phone but it didn't last. I caved as soon as we reached the meerkats. I mean, they're *meerkats!* Their little hands! Their little faces! And there was this baby one that kept toppling over!

(As a side note, I've been begging for a pet meerkat since I was two, but the California Code of Regulations, Title 14, Division 1 of the Fish and Game Commission keeps telling me no.)

Anyway, Dad was right. You're never too old for the zoo. As much as I wanted to be bored, my inner dork kept getting in the way. There was just so much to learn. Plus, between all the tigers, polar bears and other creatures that technically had no business in the middle of a large city, I failed to see any dragons. Which was good.

ONE HUNDRED FIFTY-EIGHT DAYS

DAY ONE OF JUNIOR YEAR.

I'd been dreading this Wednesday for a while, and not just for the usual "school sucks" reasons, but because I hated all the "how was your summer" questions. Everyone else was always bubbling with answers of, "Oh my God, I did this, I did that, and you know what? Big wave surfing isn't as hard as it looks!" But I had no such tales of adventure. The only thing I could mention was my dragon sighting, but I'd recently decided to take that one to the grave. It sounded way too weird when I said it out loud. Heck, *you're* probably thinking I sound like a weirdo too.

After Mom dropped me off in front of the school, I made my way to Mr. Sato's Chemistry classroom. I was still ten minutes early, and I knew the gang would all be there. It wasn't that they were super into chemistry or anything, it was just that Mr. Sato left his door open, so all the Chess Club, Mathletes, and Speech & Debate kids could hang out there during breaks. This essentially made it the unofficial hub of Stafford High geekdom, and thus my unofficial home.

I spotted Sid and Thu standing outside the door in a little circle with a handful of Mathletes. I always felt awkward joining a group in mid-conversation—even if I knew everyone—so Sid always loudly proclaimed my arrival as soon as I walked up. It was actually pretty cool of him. It prevented me from defaulting to my natural state of social invisibility.

"Chloe!" he boomed.

"Why, hello Siddhartha," I said, doing a little curtsy. "Top of the morning to you." (I have no idea why I did the curtsy, but it seemed like the thing to do.)

Sid bowed in return, his eyes sparkling with excitement. "Did you hear the news?" he asked.

"What news?"

Thu lunged at him and cupped her hand over his mouth. "Don't!" she shouted.

"What news?" I said.

Sid did his best to scramble out of reach, but tiny Thu could be quite tenacious at times—just like *moi*.

"About Thu and Dawson's Creek," Sid said, laughing and swatting her hands away. "They're in love."

"*What?*"

"No we're not!" Thu screeched, attacking him with a flurry of fists. She'd given up trying to silence him though. Anyone who truly knew Siddhartha Patel would know that keeping him quiet was an impossibility.

"The truth was uncovered yesterday afternoon," Sid explained, keeping his guard up. "Our very own Tad Prescott,"—he pointed to one of the Mathletes in our circle who proudly raised his hand—"was playing Call of Duty at Dawson's Creek's house yesterday, when he accidentally glanced through one of his desk drawers."

"To steal a vape," Tad interjected.

"That's right, to steal an electronic cigarette," Sid said, swiping away Thu's hand again. "When instead of finding strawberry flavored nicotine, he found a love letter addressed to our little friend here written by the lovable bad boy of Capeside, a.k.a. Pacey Witter, a.k.a. Dawson's Creek."

"It was *not* a love letter!" Thu insisted.

Tad took a folded piece of binder paper from his pocket. "Shall I read it again?" he asked.

"NO!" Thu jumped at him, grabbing for the letter. Unfortunately for her, Tad was tall, so all he had to do was hold it out of reach. That didn't stop her from trying to climb him like a palm tree though.

Poor Thu. She looked so desperate. I felt horrible for her. I really did. She was one of my best friends in the whole world, and I knew that she was shy, and I knew how incredibly embarrassed she was right now. Her cheeks were like turnips—it was terrible.

But I had to see that letter.

"Come on guys," I said seriously. "Don't be mean! It's not like *she* wrote it. Put it away."

Tad looked at me, puzzled, while Thu continued scrambling for the note. His eyes sort of said, "*Really?*" so I answered with my own, saying "*No. Not really. Show it to me later.*"

He grinned and nodded in understanding. (I could say a lot with a look apparently.)

After the bell rang, we all split up to find our classes. My first was English with Mr. Chamberlin. But who cares about *that?*

I knew there was something going on between Dawson's Creek and Thu! I'd suspected it for months. The only reason I hadn't said anything was that if Sid heard about it, he'd harass the pair of them until they spontaneously combusted. (Which, I suppose, was what was going to happen now.) Still, there was a terrific pride in realizing my romantic Spidey Sense was right all along. Thu and Dawson's Creek—they'd actually make a really cute couple. All they had to do now was survive everyone else.

Once classes began, time dragged. I knew I should have been paying attention to, like, the teachers and stuff, but instead, I focused on little random things. Like how the secondhand in English *ticked* around the dial, while the one in Trigonometry *oozed*. I also conducted thorough scans of all my classes to see who was in them. I spotted a few friendly faces, but there was only one that I was truly looking for: Adam Worley.

It was completely absurd that I liked him. I mean, talk about your all-time, no-shot-in-heck crushes. Adam Worley was like the primo, popular hot guy, and not just for the Junior class, but for all classes in all schools in all the world. And no, that was not my opinion. That was a fact.

I'd been getting butterflies around him since middle school, and I'd never told a single soul. Not Sid, not Thu, not Dawson's Creek, no one. I knew if I did, it would only be a matter of time until they concocted some evil scenario where I'd have to actually talk to him and then, consequently, melt into a puddle.

Plus, there was the dorky embarrassment factor. I was a short, sci-fi loving geek girl (and proud of it), and he was a dreamy superhero on the lacrosse team. *The lacrosse team!* I mean, how clichéd could I be? I wasn't supposed to like guys like him, and he definitely wasn't supposed to like girls like me—which, of course, he probably didn't. Still, I couldn't help it. The heart wants what the heart wants. You can't fight true love. Destiny finds us wherever we… okay fine, I'll just admit it. The guy was fraking gorgeous. (*Battlestar Galactica* reference there, for those of you who don't know.)

Also, as a minor impediment, he already had a girlfriend—Melissa Reinhardt. She was Jason's female equivalent of off-the-charts hotness, mirroring his lacrosse stick with her pom-poms, and his abs with her magnificent boobs. (How did she *get* those things anyway?)

And she was evil too. The stories abounded. She ruined lives with a single smirk. She felled empires with a toss of her golden locks. She devoured the souls of orphaned kittens for breakfast. *And* she was really into yoga and passionately cared about the environment. Go figure.

Anyway. After my first four classes, it was time for lunch. Unlike most schools that you see in the movies, Stafford High was an outdoor campus so there wasn't a giant cafeteria where everyone sat according to popularity. Instead, everyone just scattered across a large, grassy quad.

But make no mistake—the quad was no simple landscape. The whole area brimmed with social complexity and territorial boundaries. To start, there were four distinct zones for freshmen, sophomores, juniors and seniors. The freshmen and sophomores divided themselves along a wide set of steps leading into the quad, while the juniors sat beneath a bunch of trees at the far end. The seniors—because they're so awesome it seems—sat in the very center of everything, clustered around this giant, ancient tree stump. (It served as a de facto throne, I suppose.)

But those zones only meant something if you were in the In Crowd. For the rest of us, the seating possibilities were more varied. There was Mr. Sato's classroom, which was mostly dominated by the Chess Club; there was the actual cafeteria that no one ever entered because it was a genuinely scary place (I'm not sure why); there was a corner of the quad with a smattering of benches that was open to whoever got there first; there was the general area around the vending machines, which were typically surrounded by amateur extortionists; and there was this little brick wall opposite the Juniors' trees, which was where my friends and I tended to sit. (Unless it was raining, and then Mr. Sato's was the place to be.) We'd named our spot Brick Wall Place after Thu had watched an episode of *Downton Abbey* and gotten inspired. It had a sort of "English countryside" sound to it. Or at least, so she thought.

Anyway, today was sunny, so Brick Wall Place was where I found everyone. I'd just come from Spanish 2 with Ms.

Freudenberger, who—let's admit—had a decidedly Germanic name for a Spanish teacher. For the whole class, she spoke nothing but her non-native language, which no one (even me, who studied!) understood, and then sent us on our way with an overly cheerful "*hasta luego!*" and a giant pile of homework.

As I walked up to my friends, I saw that Thu was already chasing Sid in a circle—and not just to stop him from blabbering anymore. From the look on her face, I'm pretty sure her intent was to beat him up.

I stepped over to Tad Prescott who was busy watching while eating some chips. I poked him and asked, "What's going on?"

For a second he looked startled, like he hadn't realized I was there. (Sneak Attacks: one of the benefits of being tiny.)

"Well..." he said, pausing for a moment to take a deep breath. "Apparently it went down like this: Thu, Sid and Dawson's Creek were all in second period together. Dawson's Creek was not yet aware that I'd stolen his letter, so he sat next to Thu, acting his usual self. He even said 'hi' to her, I think. Meanwhile, Sid had a picture of the letter on his phone, and he texted it to Dawson's Creek, who then stiffened up like a guilty man in church. Sid then texted Thu that he sent the letter to Dawson's Creek. And then he texted Dawson's Creek that he texted Thu, saying something like, 'Yes. She knows,' and then to her, saying, 'Yes. He knows you know," and so on for the entire class until the bell rang and they both exploded."

"Jeez," I breathed. "That must have been awkward."

"Like a Nazi at a Bar Mitzvah."

"So where's Dawson's Creek?" I asked. "Shouldn't he be the one beating up Sid? Or *you,* for that matter?"

Tad shook his head. "No one's heard from him since. There's a rumor that he walked off campus and never came back."

I took a couple of Tad's chips and watched Thu jump on Sid's back, pounding on the top of his head with her fist. As far as I was concerned, he deserved it. I thought about joining her—just for the fun of beating up a boy, which in Sid's case was very possible—but thought better of it. I wasn't exactly in the greatest shape at the moment, and I didn't want to collapse from heat exhaustion or something.

And then, right as I was thinking that, I saw *it* again. No one else did, of course, but I saw it clear as day—circling overhead like a giant hawk. It even let out a horrible screech. I suddenly felt like Dawson's Creek must have felt right after getting that first text message. A secret had been exposed. I went totally stiff, as everyone around me seemed to fade into the background. To them, everything was still normal. Tad was still eating his chips. Thu and Sid were still fighting. A small crowd was still cheering them on.

But me? No. I was staring up at the sky at a dragon that apparently no one else could see.

ONE HUNDRED FIFTY-EIGHT & ONE HALF DAYS

ADMITTEDLY, IT'S NOT EASY to see a dragon twice in one week and then go on with the rest of your day…

But I was determined to try.

My next class was—okay, you know what? It actually wasn't *that* weird. I've been imagining all sorts of completely unreasonable things since I was a zygote. Talking ponies. Life-sized Pokémon. Klingon tea parties. All in all, a dragon barely registered. Perfectly normal—Physics with Mr. Bowen. Like anyone else, I'd heard about him. He was the most famous teacher at Stafford, and when I stepped into his classroom, I suddenly understood why.

Basically, imagine a guy whose airplane had crash-landed in the middle of the Alaskan wilderness and he's just spent the past nine months surviving with nothing but a pocketknife and a shoelace. That's *exactly* how Mr. Bowen looked. His long, matted brown hair resembled the aftermath of a tiny explosion on his scalp; his beard was big enough to house a full family of birds; and his eyes were wild, like he was seeing everything for the very first time. And he was a *Physics* teacher.

Now, here's the thing about me: I *love* science. Everything about it. When you're a scientist the entire universe becomes a giant puzzle and your job is to *solve it*. I mean, how cool is that?? The answer: Very cool. So it goes without saying that I was excited about my first foray into the wide world of physics, and definitely eager to see what Mr. Mountain Man had in store for us.

I took a seat at the last remaining empty desk and got out my spiral notebook. I'd decorated it the night before. It had Albert Einstein superimposed on the bridge of the *U.S.S. Enterprise*, pointing straight ahead and barking, "Make it so!"

The desks—which all had plenty of surface area for experiments I noted—had two chairs apiece and were arranged in a large circle around the room. In the center was a large, homemade-looking trampoline. Next to it was Mr. Bowen, busily rummaging through a pile of bags at his feet.

When the bell rang he shot straight up (like a meerkat!), completely bewildered that anyone else was there.

"You're here!" he boomed, sounding genuinely shocked. "Marvelous how that works! So! Welcome! I'm Mr. Bowen. As for your names, I'll figure them out over the next several months. But first things first: Who can tell me what 'gravity' is?"

There was a shimmer of nervous delay before someone finally raised their hand. It was a giant senior I recognized from the Jock Crowd named Wesley Cooper. "It's, uh, what makes things fall," he said.

"Yes!" Mr. Bowen exclaimed. "That's exactly what it is! But it's also more. Anyone else?"

Another delay. A girl in my year raised her hand. "Isn't it like Isaac Newton's thing? It pulls things to the ground?"

Again, Mr. Bowen's eyes lit up. "Yes! And?"

Okay, now was my moment. Ever since kindergarten, I tended to be *a bit* of a teacher's pet, and one way to continue this trend was to secretly google the answers to questions on my phone.

I confidently raised my hand. "Gravity," I said, "is a natural phenomenon by which all things with energy are brought toward one another."

Whipping around, Mr. Bowen's face lit up like a Christmas tree. "Ah! A fellow Wikipedia lover! I've read that one myself. Now if memory serves... skip to the second paragraph."

My cheeks flushed. He'd *memorized* the article on gravity?

"Go ahead," he prompted as I paused. "No need to hide the phone under your desk. I'm going to have you guys use them all the time. Paragraph Two is fascinating."

Okay then...

I cleared my throat, suddenly feeling a rather large lump in it as everyone stared at me. "Gravity," I began reading, "is most accurately described by the General Theory of Relativity proposed by Albert Einstein in 1915, which describes gravity not as a force but as a consequence of the curvature of spacetime caused by the uneven distribution of mass/energy; and resulting in gravitational time dilation, where time lapses more slowly in lower gravitational potential. Um... should I keep going?"

"Oh, if it were up to me, *yes*. Big time yes. But unfortunately we all happen to be traveling far slower than the speed of light so time is limited. Hence, *time dilation*. So..." He rotated to look around the room. "I heard a couple cool things in there. General Theory of Relativity and Spacetime. Anyone know what those are?"

Silence.

"Excellent," Mr. Bowen said. "Then all the time I spent sowing together this trampoline from my old gym shorts didn't go to waste."

And then began one the coolest demonstrations I'd ever seen. With nothing more than a trampoline, a bowling ball and a handful of marbles, Mr. Bowen showed us exactly how the General Theory of Relativity worked, as well as what gravity truly was. Basically, the trampoline was "spacetime," the bowling ball was the Sun, and the marbles were planets. He placed the bowling ball at the center causing the latex to sag in the middle. Then he tossed the marbles onto the fabric at an angle, and they immediately went into orbit, just like the solar system. Small marbles would even orbit the bigger ones like moons around planets. Eventually someone asked why all the planets orbited in the same direction, so he tossed two handfuls in opposite directions. Within a couple orbits one side eliminated the other until everything was going the same way. All the while, Mr. Bowen's excitement only increased.

"So who's heard of dark energy?" he asked, grabbing a plastic pipe from his bag. "Sounds like science fiction, right? But it's not. It's the invisible force that makes the universe expand. Watch this!" He dove under the spandex and propped up the pole in the middle, forming a little tent. "See?" He scrambled back to his feet. "Now the marbles roll *away* from each other! Dark energy!"

I was just about to join everyone else in a collective, "whoa!" when something extraordinary caught my eye—a sudden movement in the open doorway. A lone figure, tall and broad of shoulder.

"Uh, hey," the figure said, grabbing everyone's attention. "I guess I went to the wrong room? I think I'm in this class."

I stared at this cosmic anomaly for what seemed an eternity. How could this be happening to me? My heart was beating all the way up in my nose. I could feel it in my ears. *Thump. Thump. Thump.*

"The more the merrier!" Mr. Bowen exclaimed. "Come on in. Take a seat."

And so Adam "Oh My God" Worley, complete with lacrosse stick and gym bag, strode in and took the last remaining seat… *right next to me.*

He nodded casually.

I stared back, blank-faced.

So much for learning a single, stupid thing this semester. And my notebook... oh no. I immediately flipped it over. Did he see it? I bet he *did*. I bet he's thinking "what a dork," even as we speak! Or does he like Albert Einstein? Or Jean-Luc Picard? That'd be nice. But improbable. Definitely need to redecorate. Maybe I'll find something cool like a Klingon *Bird of Pre*— no.

Curse you, Love of Star Trek!!!

• • •

So after roughly forty-three minutes and nineteen seconds of heart-pounding, love-struck, adrenaline-induced panic, Physics was over. My last class for the day was Drama 1. Sid was in it, and as I steadily worked at calming my nerves, he orbited around me like one of the marbles on Mr. Bowen's trampoline.

Our Drama teacher, meanwhile, simply told us to "do whatever you like" as she sat in a crumbled heap near the back of the room. She was really young, like in her twenties or something, but looked like an absolute train wreck. She kept massaging her temples and taking long drinks from a thermos.

She didn't tell us her name either, but the one thing I did notice was that she had a thick English accent. Which was cool, but... well, the class was a bit of a let down. Like Physics, Drama was one of the things I liked. I'd always figured that if my plans for becoming a professional treasure hunter didn't pan out, then being an international star of stage and screen would suffice. I'd even drawn up detailed plans. And Drama 1, though not essential, was a small piece of those plans.

Oh well.

ONE HUNDRED
FIFTY-SEVEN DAYS

THE NEXT DAY at school was pretty much like the first: boring in the first half, awkward in the middle, and okay at the end. In Drama there was a substitute teacher who had us watch a movie. It was Joss Whedon's *Much Ado About Nothing*, which obviously I'd already seen like a million times. (Agent Coulson is in it!)

After school I went to Sid's house for a study session, but even for us, it was a tad early for much studying. Mostly all I had was a bunch Spanish homework from Ms. Freudenberger.

"Are you getting these texts?" Sid asked, bounding back into his room after spending an inordinate amount of time in the bathroom that I thoroughly did not want to think about.

"From who?" I shifted over on his floor as he plopped next to me.

"Dawson's Creek. You gotta see this." He handed me his phone with a triumphant grin.

Dawson's Creek: Dude seriously. How'd u get it?

Dawson's Creek: Did u steal it?

Dawson's Creek: It was Tad wasn't it?

Dawson's Creek: I KNOW it was him.

Dawson's Creek: That fckr.

Dawson's Creek: Dude, why aren't u answering?

Dawson's Creek: R U there?

Dawson's Creek: Was it YOU???

Dawson's Creek: Did YOU take it???!!!

Dawson's Creek: u did, didn't u?

Dawson's Creek: Tell me or I tell everyone about that girl in seventh grade.

Dawson's Creek: Janice.

Dawson's Creek: DUDE!!!! ANSWER!!!!!!!!!

Dawson's Creek: DUDE!!!!

Dawson's Creek: OK seriously. What's Thu saying?

Dawson's Creek: Is she pissed?

Dawson's Creek: Come on man, please?

Dawson's Creek: dude?

Dawson's Creek: please answer...

"I'm not sure, but I think he was crying by the end," Sid said with enormous pride.

"You're evil," I told him. "Why didn't you text him back?"

He looked at me like I was crazy. "And miss watching him go through all the stages of a meltdown via text message? No way."

I rolled my eyes and turned back to my Spanish book. "I still don't get what the big deal is. So he likes Thu. Why is that so bad?"

"Because, young Chloe, Dawson's Creek is one of the beautiful people. Did you know that Emily Sulecki likes him? *Emily Sulecki!* I heard about it last week. That girl is so hot she could split an atom by looking at it. She's the *actual* cause of global warming. You could fry an egg on her bu—"

I threw my pen at him. "I get it. And you're gross."

"Yeah." Sid shrugged. "So he's got a rep to maintain. The instant he starts publically hanging with the likes of us, all the Emily Suleckis will disappear."

"That's so lame."

Right as I said that, however, I thought about Adam Worley. Adam "Washboard Abs" Worley with his shoulders and his eyes and his hair and his smile and that little mole behind his left ear and that tangy sweet smell that I've discovered comes from the shampoo "Flex: Dark Temptation" after sampling dozens of brands at the grocery, and the way his dark eyebrows furrow when he's confused, and the way he sits (there's something about his calves!), and the way he walks, and the way he laughs, and the way my heart flutters, and...

Sid waved a hand in front of my face. "You okay?" he asked.

I instantly straightened my shoulders. "*What? * Why?"

"Well, for starters, there's a little drool hanging out of your mouth."

Crap. Indeed there was... I wiped it with the collar of my shirt. "Just thinking," I chirped.

"Uh... about?"

I paused and looked at him quizzically. Sid and I were friends, right? *Best* friends. I'd known him since forever. We were two peas in a pod. After all, it was *he and I* who'd discovered his older brother's stash of bottle rockets (as well as an alarming cache of dirty magazines) in fourth grade. It was *he and I* who'd almost burned down a neighbor's house with said bottle rockets. It was *he and I* who'd stolen Mr. Quigley's clipboard in fifth grade and run it up the school's flagpole. It was *he and I* who'd gone to middle school dances together because no one else wanted to go with us.

So... I could tell him about Adam, right? It would be nice to have a partner in crime. A confidant. But what would he do? How would he react? Would he help, or... I suddenly remembered Thu jumping on his back and punching him. I remembered her chasing him in circles. I remembered his gleeful smile as she did so. I thought of Dawson's Creek weeping in a dark room and waiting for a text. So, yeah.

Maybe I couldn't tell him. But there was always the indirect route.

"Can I... ask you a question?" I finally said.

He furrowed his brow. "Are you about to tell me you're an alien or something? Because that's about how weird you're acting right now."

"Do you..." I started to ask, then clamped my mouth shut. I studied him again.

"Do I what?"

Screw it.

"Do you think I'm pretty?" I asked.

There was a sudden lump in my throat as I felt my cheeks flush. Even asking *Sid* felt embarrassing. But in truth, it was the heavenly image of Adam's smile that flitted through my head at that moment that really got my heart beating.

"Uhhhhh..." Sid started to back away.

It took me a second to realize what he was thinking, and I quickly lunged at him. "No, no! Not like that!" I squealed. "I'm not asking in a 'do you like me' kind of way. I'm just asking, like... *objectively.* And you're my best friend so you have to be honest."

There was another brief pause before I saw a flood of relief wash across his face. "Wow," he gasped. "That was about to get real awkward. I mean, I think you're awesome and everything, but... so why are you asking me if you're pretty?"

"I just want to know."

"But why?"

Adam Worley, Adam Worley, Adam Worley, Adam Worley, Adam Worley...

I raised my nose imperiously. "Yours is not to ask why, Siddhartha. Yours is to do as I say. Girls need to know these things."

Another pause.

"So?" I asked.

Sid thought a moment and then shrugged. "You really don't know?" he asked.

"Don't know what?"

"Yes, Chloe. You are pretty."

I brightened, sitting straighter. "*Really?*"

"Well, let's put it this way: You're—wait, before I say more, I'm requesting immunity, okay? You can't get all weird on me if I say something you don't like. Deal?"

"Deal."

"Then yeah. You're more on the 'cute' side of pretty. As opposed to 'hot.' Like Emily Sulecki is *hot*, for example. But that's probably just because you always wear baggy overalls and never wear contacts."

"They sting!"

Sid held up his hands. "It's not a bad thing. It makes you… I don't know. Like the girl-next-door type."

"And that's good?"

"Sure." He shifted. "Now why in the turd nuggets are you asking me this? Do you have a crush on some guy or something?"

The ghost of Sir Laurence Olivier would've nodded approvingly at the casualness to my response. "No," I said. "Just curious."

"Well consider yourself lucky then. I know *for a fact* that I'm ugly. Remember that poll that Alison Pape took about me in eighth grade? That was harsh. I mean, empirical evidence!"

"That was stupid," I told him quickly. "You're… not ugly."

He raised an eyebrow.

"Okay fine," I said. "But you're like… I don't know. Austin Powers or something. You transcend looks."

"*Yeah baby!*"

"But don't do that."

He immediately jumped into a preposterous pose. "*Do I make you horny, baby?*" Another pose. "*Randy?*"

"Ew! I take it back! No more Austin Powers!"

"By the way," he said, switching back to his normal voice without skipping a beat. "You need to clear your schedule next Friday."

I grimaced at him. "Clear my schedule? Do you even know me? What's happening next Friday?"

"The best night of our lives, that's what."

I rolled my eyes again. Sid was always doing this. Practically every ridiculous (and memorable) thing my friends and I ever did began with a plan from Sid.

"Which means?" I asked skeptically.

"Well," he said, suddenly bashful and studying his feet. "Have you ever heard of a little band called… *Go Go Bananas?*"

I bolted upright. He wasn't serious, was he? *Go Go Bananas?!* They were my favorite band of all time! They were the best! Electronica/Punk/Hip Hop/Something Completely Original! And the *lead singer…* oh my God. Did Sid really have tickets? Did he, did he, *did he???*

"Do you—?" I began to ask.

"Have tickets?" he finished. "No. Are you crazy? Those are impossible to get."

In a heartbeat, I went from joy to fury. I grabbed my book and jumped into attack mode.

"Wait!" he cried quickly, backing away. "What I was about to say is that those are impossible to get… *if* you're a mere mortal."

I paused, book raised. "Wait," I said, eyeing him suspiciously. "So…?"

"So you, me, Thu and one more at the Fillmore next Friday at eight."

"Sid!" I wailed and instantly jumped on him. (Totally platonically.)

"Yes, I know," he said matter of factly. "I'm amazing. No need to say it."

"But how?" I asked.

"Magical powers. Plus, I have a cousin who works there."

ONE HUNDRED FIFTY-SIX DAYS

OKAY, SO HERE ARE THREE THINGS you should know: 1.) I discovered yesterday that our seating assignments in Physics are permanent. 2.) I will be sitting next to Adam Worley for eternity. 3.) I've redecorated my notebook.

I replaced *Star Trek* with album art for *Go Go Bananas*. It depicted a banana peel draped over the edge of a dumpster with a caption that read: *"This is you."*

Cool, right? Only an awesome and totally sexy girl would have such amazing taste in music, if I do say so myself.

Thus, as I waited for class to start, there was no shame whatsoever as the notebook sat proudly atop my desk. Mr. Bowen was up front fiddling with a laptop and a huge flat screen. I was so busy watching him (the man fascinated me), that I completely didn't notice Adam Worley taking his seat until I heard: "Hey, what happened to Einstein?"

Whoa.

Hold on.

At this moment, I'd like to ask you to breathe. Just press pause a moment. Stretch. Enjoy some silence. Have you done it? Okay, good. Now:

Did Adam Worley just ask me, "What happened to Einstein?" Did he just say the words like it was no biggie? Just casual conversation? "Hey Chloe, what happened to Einstein?" No. No, no, no. This wasn't casual. This was huge. This was *beyond* huge. This was the first time Adam Worley had spoken directly to me since that one time in sixth grade when I dropped my pencil. The words "here you go," have echoed ever since. And now: *"What happened to Einstein????"*

It then occurred to me that I'd been gaping silently for about ten seconds.

"Um…" I said, and then for some reason my nose started twitching like a bunny rabbit's.

Adam frowned, leaning closer. "Yeah," he said. "You had him on the bridge of the *Enterprise*. He was saying 'make it so,' like Captain Picard does."

Nope. You didn't read that wrong. Adam Worley, star lacrosse player and the hottest guy who ever lived, knew that "make it so" was the catch phrase of Captain Jean-Luc Picard on *Star Trek: The Next Generation*.

If I wasn't in love with him already, now I *really* was.

"Oh," I squeaked, then cleared my throat. "Just wanted to, um, change things up. You like *Star Trek*?"

He laughed. (*He laughed!*) "Promise you won't tell anyone?" he said, lowering his voice. "I'm actually a huge sci-fi nerd. *Star Trek, Farscape, BSG*. And *Firefly*—best show ever made."

At that moment, Adam Worley got very lucky. He didn't know it, but he was about 0.5 seconds away from getting jumped on and physically overpowered by the tiny geek girl in his Physics class. But right as that girl's muscles tensed to do so, Mr. Bowen announced, "Everyone! I've got something amazing to show you!" And the girl stood down.

"This is one of my favorite TED Talks," Mr. Bowen said, queuing up a video on the giant screen. "It's not about physics, per se, but it cuts to the very heart of science. Which is?"

Silence. I would've raised my hand but my pulse was still traveling at maximum warp.

Mr. Bowen shrugged. "Questioning things," he said. "Looking at something and saying: 'what the heck *is* that?' That's what science is all about. So without further ado…" he bent down to press play, but his computer froze. He poked at it for a minute, and then the TED Talk began.

I'll admit, I missed the first few minutes. My brain was still winding down from the endorphin overload, but eventually I got the gist. The lecturer was talking about something called "Interface Theory." His research—which used a bunch of crazy math formulas and computer simulations—suggested that reality isn't real. Like, when you open your eyes, you're brain is actually lying to you, showing you this dumbed-down version of reality so you can perform tasks better. According to him, all objects—from muffins to cars to your own reflection—are like the icons on your computer screen. They give you a user-friendly "interface" to interact with. But what reality really is? No one knows. Nuts, right?

"That's what I'm talking about," Mr. Bowen said when it was over, switching off the screen. "Interface Theory. One of the most important questions around: 'what *is* all of this?'" He gestured to everything around the room. "Why is it here? Why is there *something* rather than *nothing*? Human beings have been trying to answer that question for a real long time. So!" He ran over to a stack of papers on his desk and started passing them out. "This is what I like to call your 'Fun Final.' At the end of the semester, you'll have a regular final exam like all your other classes, but the day before, you'll also have a Fun Final. This year, that will involve finding your own TED Talk— preferably one about science—then giving a short presentation on what you learned. These handouts have a few suggested questions that will help you get started."

When Adam and I got our papers I leaned over to look at his instead of mine. (I don't know why.) The first question read: "How does this idea change things?"

ONE HUNDRED
FIFTY-TWO DAYS

A FEW DAYS LATER, I was sitting with my friends at lunch when I saw something startling. I was just beginning to wonder, "where's Thu?" when I saw her marching solo across the quad—her mouth a grim line of determination.

At first, I thought she was on her way to try her luck with the vending machines, but no. Her trajectory was off. It wasn't candy bars she was after. It was Dawson's Creek.

I poked Sid, who was busily talking to Tad through a mouthful of peanut butter and jelly sandwich. "Hey," I said to him. "This doesn't look good."

He looked over. "Wha oesn't?" he asked, trying to swallow. I pointed.

"Oh." He gulped. "This won't go well at all."

"Should we try to stop—?"

"Too late," he cut me off. "She's reached her objective."

We both silently watched. Dawson's Creek was sitting amidst his cool friends beneath the trees. Thu stood a few feet away, her arms locked at her sides. Her back was to us, so I couldn't see what was happening. Eventually, however, a number of faces turned toward her. Then a peel of laughter began, which included Dawson's Creek. Abruptly, Thu did a military-style about face and ran away. There were tears on her cheeks as her long hair billowed behind her. I couldn't tell where she was going, but it didn't matter. Sid and I were instantly on our feet. We caught up to her by the open benches where she'd collapsed onto the metal and buried her face in her lap. I'd never seen her cry so hard. Slowly, I sat and put my arms around her while Sid knelt in front of us. "Hey," he said to her quietly. His tone was serious—something that only happened on very rare and special occasions. "I'm sorry, Thu. Really."

She kept her face down, her back heaving with heavy sobs. "It's not your fault," she said between gasps. "I was never mad at *you*. Not really."

"What did he say?" I asked.

"He's such a jerk," she spat. "I just asked him if we could talk!"

I hugged her tighter and she continued. "He said, '*Uh, do I know you?*' And then all his stupid friends started laughing."

Sid winced. "Damn."

Thu's head snapped up. Her face was a mess—swollen and tear-soaked. "You guys don't understand!" she burst. "I *loved* him! We made out! A lot!"

"Really?"

"Yes really! But now it's like he's a different person!"

Sid's earlier explanation about Dawson's Creek's "cool guy" reputation flashed through my head. But honestly, that didn't make sense. I knew Dawson's Creek better than that. We all did. He was our friend. There had to be a better reason.

"He's being a boy," I told Thu. "And as we all know, boys are the stupidest creatures on the planet."

"We are," Sid agreed. "Very much so."

"But—"

"It's a mathematical fact." I nuzzled her with my forehead. "Plus, me and Sid are going to talk to him. And if diplomacy fails—war."

Thu groaned and reburied her face in her hands. "This is so embarrassing."

"No." Sid shook his head. "When Dawson's Creek shows up at school next week with no eyebrows—*that* will be embarrassing."

Thu let out a choked laugh, trying not to smile. "Don't do that," she said.

We stayed with her until the bell rang. She told us all about how she and Dawson's Creek got started when he gave her a ride home from a D&D game, and how amazing it had been the past couple months. She really *loved him*. It wasn't just some crush. And by the way she told the story, it sounded like he'd really loved her too. But now? He was being a complete and utter dummy.

ONE HUNDRED FIFTY-ONE DAYS

THE NEXT DAY I was sitting with Thu and Sid at lunch. Thu seemed to be doing better, which probably had something to do with Sid's constant efforts to cheer her up. You should've seen him, dancing around and even *juggling* at one point like he was in the circus.

But me? I felt horrible. Like *physically* horrible. I was pretty sure I was getting the flu. My whole body ached and the world was spinning around me like a giant top. Every few minutes I had to stop myself from gagging, which as you probably know, is one of the worst feelings on Earth. I should've just gone to the nurse, but I didn't want to. The thought scared me somehow. I felt like if I just pretended everything was normal, then eventually it would be.

But it hurt. It hurt really, really bad.

So when I looked up and saw it, I wasn't even surprised. It was sitting on the roof like it had been there all along. Wings folded. Weight on its haunches. It was staring right at me. Those big, snake-like eyes.

Crap, I thought miserably. *I'd almost forgotten about that.*

ONE HUNDRED FIFTY DAYS

EVENTUALLY, THAT GROSS "I'm gonna puke" feeling decided to leave and the timing couldn't have been better. Our Drama teacher was finally back. She explained her absence as a "bit of a life crisis," and kept repeating that she was "so, so sorry." (Her accent was *awesome* by the way, and I made a quick note to study my Britishisms.)

"My name is Miss Collins," she said after her profuse apology. She then frowned at herself. "Gosh. It sounds rather strange to say that. *Miss* Collins. My given name is *Poppy*, actually. But I'm afraid here in America that sounds a bit odd, doesn't it?"

A peel of laughter confirmed her suspicions.

"Figured as much," she said. "Miss Collins it is."

Sid, sitting next to me, immediately raised his hand. "Do you have a boyfriend?" he asked.

There was another round of laughter and I elbowed him. Why did he always have to say things like that? Was it genetic? Although, on second thought, I knew exactly what he was up to. He was being stupid for three reasons: 1.) He was a boy, 2.) Miss Collins was ridiculously gorgeous (or "hot," as he would say), and 3.) The original hot girl, Emily Sulecki, was in our class and he was showing off. Miss Collins, meanwhile, didn't seem perturbed in the slightest. Instead, she immediately fired back, "No. Do you?"

For a brief moment, Sid actually looked flustered, "Uh, no?" he said.

Then the impossible happened. He didn't say anything else! No comeback! No pithy remark. How did she *do* that? Was it the accent?

"Right then," Miss Collins said with a curt nod. "I thought we'd begin today's lesson with an audition of sorts. So…" She eyed the room and then stuck out her hand like she was directing traffic. "Okay, this half of the room—zombies. This other half—not zombies. Got it? Good. Now *act!*"

Just like numerous moments in Mr. Bowen's class, there was a shimmer of nervous delay. Did she mean, "act like zombies?" Like, *right now?*

I slowly stood from my seat, raised my arms and gave Sid a dead stare. He stared back in confusion until he caught on and did the same. Soon, the whole class was groaning and chasing and screaming. It was chaos. Some of the non-zombies pushed over desks and erected a barricade. Some of the zombies started attacking each other. Others got organized and mounted an assault. Sid, I noticed, went after Emily Sulecki (a non-zombie) and chased her in circles around the room. She looked genuinely terrified.

Meanwhile, Miss Collins was taking notes. *A lot* of notes. She seemed particularly interested in whatever Sid was doing.

Finally, she stood in the middle of the fray and held up her hands. "Time!" she cried. "Audition is over!"

A final, zombie-like groan answered her. "Back to you seats," she said, smiling. "Although it looks like we will have to dismantle the barricade first."

Once that was done, Miss Collins got back to the front of the room. "As you all know," she announced, "every year the Drama class puts on a fall play. Usually it's something boring by Shakespeare or Arthur Miller. This year will be different. This year we'll be putting on a play that's yet to debut anywhere in the world. It's a comedy and quite short—written by myself, as well as my very talented yet horrendously atrocious ex-husband—which we won't discuss any further—and its title is, *Zombie Apocalypse: A Love Story.*"

Half the class, including me, couldn't help but laugh. Miss Collins had said the title so seriously, she made it funny. See? *Britishisms.*

"Now," she said, regaining our attention. "I've already decided on the three leads. The male lead will be the young man who was so interested in my relationship status. What is your name?"

Sid looked up, startled. "Sid?" he said.

"Sid," she repeated. "Cheers. You're the lead. And your co-star is the young lady you were so keen on chasing round the room."

My eyes instantly went to Emily Sulecki who, once again, looked genuinely terrified. Sid, on the other hand, lit up like a firework display. He really *was* like Austin Powers. (Except with much better teeth.)

But poor Emily. She didn't know what was coming. The force of nature that is Siddhartha Patel was about to enter her life whether she liked it or not. I didn't know whether to pity her or be happy for Sid. Maybe both?

"Now," Miss Collins said sharply. "As for our lead zombie, I want *you.*"

I scanned the room until I realized her eyes had fallen directly on me. I bolted upright.

"Me?" I squeaked.

"You," she said.

ONE HUNDRED FORTY-NINE DAYS

"CHLOE, ARE YOU REALLY SURE you want to do this?"

"MOM!" I yelled at her for the hundredth time. She was downstairs shouting up to me while I frantically tore through every piece of clothing I owned. "We've been over this!"

Selecting the right outfit was an extremely delicate affair. Tonight was the night of *Go Go Bananas*, but as far as my parents knew, it was just another "Friday Night? Game Night!"

I'd told them we were doing it at Thu's house, and that I was going to sleep over when we were done. (I felt bad about lying sort of, but… well, it was *Go Go Bananas*.)

Mom's voice was muffled as she answered back, "I know, but… can I at least get you to take some healthier snacks?"

I shot a look at my door as if it were her. We did this a lot: long distance conversations between the upstairs and downstairs.

"Cheetos and Mountain Dew are a sacred tradition!" I shouted, grabbing a new top from a previously discarded pile.

"But we can pick you up at midnight if you want. It's really okay."

"MOM!"

God, my hair was a nightmare. Some nights the frizz monster simply refused to be tamed. Technically, I had a wide assortment of industrial strength scrunchies for such occasions, but this was not a Scrunchie Night. This was a "The-Lead-Singer-For-Go Go Bananas-Might-Glance-In-My-Direction Night." Or better yet, this was a "Despite-The-Transformers-Logo-On-My-Book-Bag-I-Actually-Do-Have-Boobs Night."

The trick, however, was that my eagle-eyed parents couldn't suspect any of this. I needed to look normal, yet *awesome*. I grabbed another top.

"Chloe," Mom called again. "I think Sid is here, honey."

"Stall him!"

A brief silence answered back before she shouted, "But he makes me uncomfortable!"

I couldn't help but smile at that. Since the age of ten, Sid has had zero reservations about telling my mom how hot he thinks she is. Even the fact that she could probably lift him over her head like a toy hasn't slowed him down. If anything, it's encouraged him.

I took a final look in the mirror. It wasn't perfection, but it was the best I could do.

Hmm, I thought, turning appraisingly. *Sexy Tomboy. That's a look, right?*

Yes. It *was* a look. Jean shorts. American Apparel top. Flannel over shirt. Rolled up sleeves. Lots of bracelets. Pink Converse. Hair… well, not everything can be a victory.

I grabbed my bag and ran down the stairs to find Sid leaning against the doorframe and casually complimenting Mom's yoga pants. "What is this material?" he was asking, reaching to touch it. She literally had to swat his hand away.

"Sid," I said plainly. (Plain was my tone for letting him know it was time to stop flirting.)

He flashed me a devilish grin. "Took you long enough," he said. "It's just Dungeons and Dragons, weirdo. No need to get dressed up."

My eyes flashed, but I clamped my mouth shut. Mom looked between us and then reluctantly handed me a bag of Cheetos. "I thoroughly disapprove of these," she said. "You sure you don't want us to pick you up?"

I glared at her. (She was really making this "lying about where I'm going" thing difficult.) "I'm sure," I said, then turned to Sid with my chin jutted. "And I'm not dressed up. I'm trying out new looks."

"Well," he said, gesturing to the door. "Vera awaits. Mrs. Cartwright, you're always welcome to come with us…"

I elbowed him. "Mom, I'll call you tomorrow morning."

I started pushing Sid toward the door as my mom forced a smile. "Not too late though, okay honey? You should set your phone for seven."

Ugh…

"Will do," I said. "Bye!"

And with that, I was out the door.

• • •

After six months of riding in Sid's car, I'd never gotten used to the smell. It was a stale blend of dirty socks, baby wipes, tropical fruit, toothpaste, cigarettes and some other aroma that couldn't be named. His response to this—if anyone ever mentioned it—was that the smell "gives her character."

And of *course* his car was a she. He'd named her Vera. And if you're really, really, really cool, you'll know where that name comes from. (But in case you're not, Vera is the name of Jayne Cobb's giant, ridiculous-looking gun on the show *Firefly*.)

Basically, Vera was the ugliest automobile ever driven. She began her life in the early 1990s as a maroon Plymouth minivan. Since then, she'd lost every last scrap of her original paint and most of her upholstery. Duct tape covered everything, including a couple of the windows. Plus, and most disconcertingly, the engine made this whining sound that was eerily similar to the cartoonish whistle a bomb makes when it falls from the sky.

"So," Sid said, turning down the music a little before resuming his drumming on the steering wheel. "Who's ready to go, go bananas?"

Thu and I shared a glance.

"Dude, was that a pun?" Tad Prescott asked from the front seat. (He was so tall, it would've been cruel to call shotgun.)

"If it is, I didn't make it," Sid answered. "What else could the name mean?"

"According to Wikipedia," I noted, "the name *Go Go Bananas* refers to a nefarious strip club in Amsterdam."

Tad whipped around a little too fast. "What makes it nefarious?"

"The article didn't say," I answered. "And you know why? Because some questions are better left unanswered, perv."

"Speaking of which," Sid said. "What do you guys think about my chances with Emily Sulecki?"

We answered him with a long silence before bursting into laughter. Eventually, Tad looked at him. "Dude. If you're referring to the same Emily Sulecki that I think you are, then… I don't know. Zero?"

Thu laughed and looked up from her phone. "Sid, why would you even ask that?"

"Emily is going to be Sid's co-star in the fall play," I explained. "They're going to be zombie lovers."

"We're not *zombies*," Sid scoffed. "Didn't you read the script?"

"We got it yesterday."

"I've read it twice," he said proudly. "*Zombie Apocalypse: A Love Story* is going to be bigger than *Cats*. It's about a guy and a girl on their first date—like dinner and a movie and stuff—and they're so into each other that they don't notice the zombie apocalypse happening all around them. Like throughout the whole play, they're walking around and flirting while there's all this, like, carnage in the background. And *you*, young Chloe, play the main zombie that's trying to get them, but you keep missing."

Thu shrugged and went back to her phone. "Sounds weird," she said. "How could they possibly not notice?"

"Love," Sid answered.

Another silence. I then informed him that that was incredibly cheesy.

"I second that," Tad said. "And I still maintain that your chances with Emily Sulecki are zero. Or less than zero if that's possible."

"Shows what you know." Sid held his nose in the air. "Romance between co-stars is a time-honored tradition. You'll see."

• • •

I'd never been to the Fillmore before. On the outside, it was just a big, brick building like a zillion others in San Francisco. On the inside, it was a time machine. Every square molecule was plastered with old poster art from the sixties with swirly psychedelic letters and saturated neon colors. Bright crystal chandeliers, like relics from some decadent French palace, hung from the ceiling, while colored spotlights and lasers lit up the smoke-drenched stage. And if there was one word that could sum up the whole place, that word was "red." Everything glowed with it—like this deep, crimson hue that had soaked itself into the air.

Bananas fans were everywhere and the theater was packed. The opening band was already playing, but I'd never heard of them. "*Johnny's Popsicle*," said the poster outside. They actually weren't bad.

"Who wants drinks?" Sid shouted as we maneuvered into the balcony section.

It was only slightly less crowded than the giant crunch of people on the main floor. We all raised our hands as we grabbed an open table with a foursome of stools.

"Well, I'm not going solo," he said. "I volunteer Tad to come with me."

With that, the boys left to go brave the lines. I sat with Thu and noticed she still had her nose glued to her phone. She'd been staring at it obsessively ever since we picked her up.

"Who are you texting?" I yelled into her ear.

She looked startled. "What? Oh, nobody."

My eyes narrowed.

"What?" she said.

"Thu! You haven't taken your eyes off your phone all night!"

She glanced at it again and then back at me. Her eyes had taken on a distinctly puppy dog appearance. Desperate.

"Are you okay?" I shouted.

"I…" she started to say, and then suddenly looked like she might cry.

"Thu, what's wrong?" I scooted closer.

Her face lowered resignedly and she mumbled, "I texted him."

I could barely hear her over the music. All I really heard was "him," but I pieced it together.

"Who?" I asked. "Wait—*Dawson's Creek??*"

Her head sprang back up. "I couldn't help it!"

"Thu!"

"I know!" she cried. "I just… I thought he'd text me back!"

"What did you say to him?"

"You'll hate me if I tell you."

"Thu!"

"Fine! I told him that I still love him more than anything and need to talk to him!"

Okay. So now might be a good time to tell you a quick story about Thu. In seventh grade we had this pop quiz about *The Adventures of Tom Sawyer*. (An awesome book, by the way.) Our teacher, Mr. Orloff, gave her an A-, saying that one of her answers was wrong. Thu disagreed. She insisted that the character Amy Lawrence was Tom's true love interest and not Becky Thatcher. But Orloff wouldn't budge. So she went to the principle. He wouldn't help. She went to her parents. They laughed. After that, she wrote a letter to the board of education, the school superintendent, and eventually her congresswoman. When no one responded, she took the bus downtown and forced her way into the congresswoman's office, reportedly using a backhanded slap to disable a meddlesome intern. The next day she returned to class with a signed letter from the honorable Janet Martinez, U.S. Representative for the 19th District of California, saying that yes, Amy Lawrence could in fact be considered Tom Sawyer's love interest.

Mr. Orloff changed the grade.

That was Thu Pham. She didn't give up easily.

"You actually wrote that you *love him more than anything?*" I squealed. "In a *text?* And he never texted back??"

"No!"

"That's it," I fumed. "I'm texting him."

"Don't!"

I swatted her hand away as I got out my phone. "He's being stupid," I shouted. "I'm banning him from Dungeons and Dragons for life!"

"That will crush him!"

"Who will get crushed?" Sid asked, returning with a round of Mountain Dews. He and Tad both hopped up on stools next to Thu. "We're not talking about Dawson's Creek are we?"

"NO!" Thu screamed.

Sid furrowed his brow in shock. "I'll take that as a yes," he said.

He and I exchanged a look and he dropped the subject. In fact, he was remarkably adept at changing it. He said, "So what are everyone's thoughts on the Bretton Woods Conference of 1944? Good thing? Bad thing? What do you think, Chloe?"

I briefly considered a lengthy response regarding the International Monetary Fund—I'd recently watched a fascinating YouTube video on how it was a very bad thing—but I was cut off when *Go Go Bananas* took the stage.

The crowd roared with excitement. All the lights went out. A slow, insistent base filled the air. It was like the beating of a giant heart, and I felt mine beating along with it. It kept building and building, and then, like a firecracker, the house lights erupted in a kaleidoscope of brilliant colors and the music started.

Now, I'm not sure how many concerts you've been to, but if you've been to at least one, then you'll know what I'm talking about. There's something special about live music. It's a totally different thing from just listening to it on your headphones. There's a connection or something. Something between the band and the audience that turns everyone into this single, magnificent thing. It's like… well, I'm super tempted to use the word "magical" right now, but I'll hold off.

Anyway. Song after song played and I danced and squealed like a maniac. I twirled and hopped and sang along. And you know what the most awesome part was? So did everyone else. Sid, Thu, Tad, and a thousand people I didn't know—we were all dancing, twirling and singing, and whatever else was happening in our lives—like Thu's heartbreak or Sid's girlfriendless existence or that stupid dragon that kept following me around—it all vanished. It was like nothing on Earth. It was… well, okay fine. It was magical.

Then a tall figure brushed past me and everything stopped. Of course, plenty of other people had bumped into me but this one was different. My nose twitched as I caught a familiar scent. (Did that make me sound like a she-wolf? "Familiar scent?") ((It's fine if it did, btw. "She-wolf" is one of my favorite words in the English language.)) Anyway, I smelled something—something spicy, tangy, sweet and a little mysterious.

It was almost like… no. It couldn't be. Well, I suppose it *could.* Nothing is impossible. Still, plenty of other people in the universe could use the same shampoo. I mean, the Flex Body Spray Company must have sold millions by now. Maybe billions. But there was no denying it. The musky fragrance of Dark Temptation was in the air. And its tall, shadowy source had a very similar build to a certain boy who already had my heart beating ten times faster than it ever should.

I looked for a place to hide. Our table was empty. I ran for it and ducked underneath. (Don't judge me, it was my first instinct.)

I stayed there for the next two songs, peering out with wide eyes. Eventually I confirmed my suspicions. Adam "Secret-Star-Trek-Nerd" Worley was here with his impossibly gorgeous girlfriend. They were only a few feet from where my friends and I had been dancing. Or actually, *I* was the only one who wasn't dancing anymore. Sid, Thu and Tad were still bobbing up and down like human pogo sticks.

By the time *Lie to Me* came on (one of my favorite songs), I clenched my fist and steeled myself. *Okay, Chloe. Get back out there. Be tough. It's not like he's going to notice you. It's too dark. It's too loud. And just look at Melissa's outfit! Goodness gracious. No. He won't even see you. Not with her looking like that out there.*

So I climbed out, took a long gulp of Mountain Dew, and asked myself "what would Aeryn Sun do?" (If you know who that is, then congratulations: You're a sci-fi nerd.) Aeryn Sun wouldn't hide under a table. She wouldn't cower. She'd… well actually, Aeryn Sun would probably start beating people up.

But still. She wouldn't hide. I marched back to my friends, heart pounding, and as if on cue, Adam glanced over. The moment lasted an eternity. There was Him. There was Me. Everything else disappeared. And just like it was no big deal whatsoever, he smiled and waved.

I, however, did not smile. I did not wave. I stared, blank-faced, until my glasses fogged up and my heart beat so fast I thought it was going to explode. *Boom, boom, boom*—it thudded in my chest. I could feel it in my face. I was as red as the Fillmore, and I couldn't help but wonder, *is this what true love feels like?* (A little cheesy, I know, but I couldn't help it!)

Unfortunately, I didn't get to think about that for very long, though. Instead, I felt something new. It changed everything in an instant. That's how sharply things can turn sometimes—from perfect to horrible in a blink. My heart was pounding like before, but in a very different way. It hurt. Every beat was like a punch. The music didn't sound like music anymore, just noise. I couldn't make it out. I couldn't think. The room was spinning. I tasted vomit in my throat. I turned back to the table, desperate. I needed to hide. Disappear.

But it was too late. I collapsed hard in the middle of the floor and hit my head. Something warm ran down my thighs. Someone screamed.

Then everything went black.

ONE HUNDRED FORTY-SIX DAYS

WHEN I WOKE UP the music was gone. In fact, wherever I was, it was eerily quite and dark. A faint beeping drifted past me. Groggily, I blinked. The room looked familiar. Then, after a moment, it looked very familiar. I'd been here several times before.

A hospital room—taupe and green with curtains and tubes and all kinds of machines. The giant clock opposite my bed read 3:56 a.m. I lifted my head (which weighed about a million pounds), and saw my dad sleeping in a nearby chair. He was a complete mess with oily hair and stubbly cheeks. It was like he hadn't moved in days. I suddenly wondered what *date* it was.

I collapsed back and closed my eyes. My body ached all over—way too much for sleep. My heart was beating faster too. I could hear it with the beeps.

So…

I guess now is as good a time as any to come clean. I haven't been *lying* to you exactly, just omitting a few key facts. They are as follows:

1.) I'm sick.

2.) It's not the flu.

3.) Well… let's skip Fact Number Three for now.

Anyway, in the movie *Point Break* (See? Things can change in an instant), Patrick Swayze has this great scene where he tells Keanu Reeves, "Life sure has a sick sense of humor, doesn't it?" Basically, his character is about three minutes away from swimming out to his doom so he can surf some giant waves in Australia and avoid the cops. But that's not important. What's important is what he's talking about. He's talking about control.

You see, as people, we all like to think we're the masters of our own fate. We make plans, we take action, and things turn out nicely. But that's not how it works. All those plans are just one big, silly illusion. You're not a master of anything, even if sometimes it seems that way. Patrick Swayze learned this when his whole world came crumbling down and his friends died. Now, I've learned it too.

Plans are pretty useless in a world where the tiniest things can alter your life in the biggest ways. For example, let's say you're some guy like my dad getting up and going to work one morning. If you stumble into the bathroom and brush your teeth a few seconds longer than usual, then you might miss a certain traffic light later on, which could spell the difference between getting into, or not getting into, a horrific car accident, *or* possibly arriving at Starbucks a minute later, thus missing out on the moment where you met your future spouse, which of course means that the kids you might have had together will never get born, and maybe one of those kids might have grown up to cure cancer, but now she won't because she doesn't exist, and then all the people who die of that stupid illness will die when they didn't need to, and if they had lived, then they might have gone on to do all sorts of other cool things that would change countless other lives with marriages and children and cured diseases, but now they won't because they're dead, and all of this horrible tragedy is because of *you* and your stupid decision to give those back molars a few extra strokes before spitting. And if you think that's all big and crazy and complicated, just remember that there are like seven billion other people on the planet and every single one of them is also brushing their teeth, as well as doing a million other things, and having this giant ripple effect on you and everyone else every single second of every single day!

So yeah. *Vaya con Dios.* As Keanu Reaves would say.

• • •

Admittedly, I was a little out of it when I first woke up. Now, the morning had arrived and with it came an army of nurses, checking and re-checking IV lines and heart rates and blood pressure and temperature and oxygen levels and a bunch of other things I didn't fully understand. They were all very, very cheerful, which I've learned is never a good sign. The basic rule of thumb is:

Grumpy Nurses = You Will Get Better

Cheerful Nurses = You're Screwed

It's not like I blamed them or anything. They were all incredibly nice people, and that's how incredibly nice people are—they try to make other people feel better. Speaking of which, my parents were both with me now. Mom had arrived at six and looked even worse than Dad in terms of the zero sleep factor. (She'd probably been up all night with Henry.)

I won't bother you with all the details of the tears and hugs and awkward laughter when they first saw I was awake. Instead, I'll give you the following recap:

1.) "CHLOE!" they both scream when my eyes open.

2.) I blush, feel guilty, start crying and repeat, "I'm sorry, I'm sorry" for several minutes.

3.) They tell me I shouldn't be.

4.) They pile on top of me like hug-happy, tear-soaked rugby players.

5.) This continues until a nurse says she needs to get a blood sample.

An hour later, I was attempting to eat some Hospital Jell-O. It tasted horrendous. (Does *anyone* like the cherry flavor?) Also, quite strangely, I had no appetite whatsoever, which was odd since I'd just spent the past two days getting all my meals through a little tube.

To help me, Mom was at my side, stroking my hair and doing her personal trainer thing. "Chloe, you can do it," she kept saying. "Just eat *half.*"

I imagined I was one of her clients at the gym and she was telling me to do one more push-up. (Or, in my case, one push-up in total.)

I was about three spoonfuls into the tiny, red cup when my oncologist strode briskly into the room. His bright white coat, contrasting sharply against his pitch black skin, practically flapped behind him like a breezy cape.

His name was Dr. Mark.

It was a complete mystery how he did it, but somehow the whole world seemed to change color whenever he entered the room. It was like everything got brighter. All the scary question marks disappeared because he had all the answers. There was literally *nothing* this man didn't know. Believe me, I'd checked. Ever since he became my doctor five years ago, I've repeatedly tried to stump him with the most random trivia questions ever conceived. He's never missed a single one. I mean, how many people know—off the top of their head with no Google help—that the little dot you put above an "i" is called a tittle? The answer? One.

Dr. Mark was smart. Like extraterrestrial smart. Like "I-Have-Absorbed-All-Human-Knowledge-Before-Heading-Home" smart. He was also tall. Like basketball player tall, which of course, he actually *was* a basketball player. Or at least, he was in college—something he frequently enjoyed reminding people about. The last thing I'll mention about him was his voice. I'd never heard anything like it. If it were any deeper, I would've been positive he was Darth Vader's long lost twin. (A *nice* twin, though.)

And with that voice, he started speaking the instant he crossed the doorway. That was his habit—never a wasted second.

"You!" he boomed, scanning through my chart with dart-like eyes as he came to stand over my bed. (His head practically grazed the ceiling.) He looked up from it and smiled. "If your labs looked any better, young lady, I'd boot you out of this place never to return."

I looked at Mom and then back at him, puzzled. "Really?" I asked.

"Absolutely," he said, grabbing a nearby stool and taking a seat. Even then, he towered over the bed. "Your vitals are as strong as a Ninja Turtle. It's uncanny."

If I could have rolled my eyes without it hurting, I would have. Instead, I scowled. "*A Ninja Turtle?*" I said. "I told you. I like sci-fi. Not kids stuff. There's a difference."

He arched an eyebrow. "Is that so?" he remarked, reaching for his phone. He flipped though some pictures with lightning speed and then handed it to me. "Check this out."

"What is—?

"That," he cut me off, "is one of the largest, best preserved, collections of Power Rangers memorabilia in the continental United States. And do you know who it belongs to? It belongs to *this guy.*" He pointed to himself in case there was any mistake.

I skipped through the pictures, perplexed. I mean, my god... he had it all. Zeltrax Dino Thunder, Captain Mutiny, Master Org and an unopened Savage Battle Pack... This was rare stuff! He even had Diabolico! Unopened! (Yeah. So I know a lot about the Power Rangers. They technically fall within the realm of science fiction though, right?) ((Sort of?)) My parents both stood up to look over my shoulder as I gasped at the sight of so much geekiness. I flipped through picture after picture. Eventually, I couldn't help but crack a smile. I said, "That's really dorky, Dr. Mark."

"Of course it is," he said proudly. "That's the whole point. You see, on all those fun Friday nights when my fellow teammates—I've told you I was a starting forward for Syracuse, right?"

I nodded.

"Yes. Well, when all my teammates were out having the time of their lives, going to parties and talking to pretty girls, I was at home studying. Studying all night long and all weekend too."

"And collecting Power Rangers," I added.

He shrugged his massive shoulders. "Everyone needs a hobby, my young apprentice. So listen." He glanced at my parents and then back at me. "While you were taking your beauty rest, I talked some things over with your mom and dad. For now, the most important thing for you to know is that you're all right. Nothing is causing too big a problem yet. Unfortunately, these little dizzy spells are likely to happen again. They might not be as bad as this one, or they might be worse. The point is that if you feel one coming, just lie down, wherever you are, and then make sure you're not alone. Call someone. Text someone. Tweet. Post. Snap. Instagram—whatever you have to do. Got it?" Dr. Mark held out his giant fist for a pound. Weakly, I gave it to him.

"That's my girl," he said, and then proceeded to retell me a bunch of the stuff he'd already explained a couple weeks ago. This included: Things to look out for. Things to make me feel better. Things to help me cope.

I did my best to listen, but the truth was I didn't really want to. (My parents, on the other hand, took furious notes.)

To me it was like I'd heard it all before, and this time around, it didn't really matter. Technically, there was a long,

Latin-sounding name for the type of cancer I had, but I didn't like it. There were two reasons for this: 1.) It was hard to pronounce, and 2.) It sounded really, really nasty, like a long pair of fangs.

Thus, I renamed it. I eventually settled on Everywhere Cancer. I mean, that's better, right? Much more pronounceable. *And* much more explanatory.

Everywhere Cancer ™ The Name Says It All.

This also explained why I wasn't taking any medications. No horrible chemo like the last time, and no other horrible pills to make me feel like a giant pile of crud. This time it was just Mom's flax seed meals and spinach-green smoothies. That was all we could do.

Which, I guess, leads us to Fact Number Three:

3.) I'm dying. And not even Dr. Mark can stop it.

ONE HUNDRED FORTY-FIVE DAYS

HERE'S ANOTHER IMPORTANT THING: If you're thinking I've been so overwhelmed with the Everywhere Cancer that I've forgotten to be completely mortified about collapsing and wetting myself in front of a whole crowd of people, you're wrong. When Sid, Thu, Tad and Dawson's Creek came to visit (and my parents finally left to give us some space), my imagination kicked into overdrive. I could see it all: A crowded concert, everyone having a good time, and then me right in the middle of it, passed out, glasses askew, and a giant wet stain on my stupid shorts that I'd spent so long agonizing over.

And then there was Adam Worley! Don't even get me started on that. Because seriously, did he see? Does he know what happened? How did he react? What did he say? What did he do? Didhehelp? Didhebreakupwithhisgirlfriendyet? Whyhasn'the??

I needed answers to all these questions and stat. I *also* needed to be very subtle about discovering them. No one could ever know about my secret crush. At least not right now. There was only so much embarrassment a girl could take in a single week, and I'd reached my limit.

"It really wasn't that bad," Sid explained as he recapped what happened. I stared up at him in earnest, willing him to tell me the part that mattered most. "Honestly, it was all dark and crowded," he went on. "And when we noticed that you weren't with—"

"OH MY GOD, JUST TELL ME!" I screamed. "DID ADAM WORLEY SEE???"

Crap. Nice one, Chloe…

They all stared in stunned silence before Sid asked, "Huh?"

"Nothing!" I said quickly. "I, er… I just meant…"

He scratched his head. "I thought you were unconscious. How did you know that—?"

"She saw him *before*, dummy," Thu interrupted.

"Yeah but do you know him or something?" Sid asked me, still looking confused.

"Dude," Tad said. "He told us that he's in her Physics class."

"No he didn't."

"Yes he did."

"I talked to him outside. He never said anything about…"

Sid's words trailed off as the little beeping heart monitor turned into a rapid-fire laser canon. Horrifying answers to embarrassing questions were blasting me from every direction. Adam Worley *did* see. Adam Worley *knew* things. Adam Worley *said* things. Adam Worley got *involved*. Adam Worley—

"Chloe, crap, are you okay?" Sid suddenly said. He'd gone from confused to hyper-worried in a microsecond. "Pacey! Go find a nurse!"

"No," I said firmly, halting Dawson's Creek in his tracks. "I'm fine. Just tell me what happened."

"But the beeping machine sounds like it's gonna explode."

I looked at it. "It always sounds like that." (It actually didn't.) "Did Adam, like, get weirded out? What happened? Tell me!"

Sid studied my face another second, then said, "Are you really sure you're okay?"

"Yes!"

"Well," he said, looking to Thu and Tad for confirmation. "He, uh, carried you downstairs. It was too loud on the balcony to call 911, so we took you with us to the lobby. I tried to carry you myself, but you were *waaaaay* too heavy."

Thu elbowed him.

"What?" he said. "I'm just saying... she's like a hundred pounds. I can't lift a hundred pounds, can you?"

"I could've done it," Dawson's Creek said. "Easy."

"Oh yeah? Well if you hadn't been acting like such a douche these past couple weeks, then you would've been there!"

"Thanks," Tad said. "I get it."

"Stop!" I squealed. "Focus!"

My voice had taken on the high-pitched trill of a frightened squirrel. "He *carried* me?" I said. "And I had, like, *pee* all over me?!"

Sid winced. "Was that what that was? Cause I didn't notice. He probably didn't either."

"I was covered in pee!"

Thu leaned in and took my hand. (She understood what was happening here.) "It was just a little bit! And he didn't care, I promise. You should have seen him, he was really worried about you."

I groaned as I tried to roll over. This whole thing was getting worse and worse! First I have Everywhere Cancer, then a Game of Thrones dragon starts following me around, then I faint in front a zillion people and then I pee on Adam Worley. I mean, what's going to happen next—a cartoon piano falling on my head? And how was I going to sit next to that boy ever again?! "Oh, hey Adam," I'll say. "Crazy concert, right? Hope your shirt doesn't smell too much like *urine* after you carried me to an ambulance. Oh yeah, and by the way, I have Everywhere Cancer. Would you like to be my boyfriend now?"

Ahhh!

You know what? Patrick Swayze really *did* say it best: "Life sure has a sick sense of humor."

It sure does, Mr. Swayze. It sure freaking does.

ONE HUNDRED FORTY-TWO DAYS

I GOT TO GO HOME a few days later. I still felt shaky, which probably owed more to lying in a hospital for a week than it did to the Everywhere Cancer. That didn't stop my parents, though. They insisted on helping me with every single step. Out of the car, through the front door, visiting Henry, into the kitchen—basically everywhere I went. They hovered like a pair of obsessed mother hens. It was nice of them I guess, but by evening, it was also a bit much. I told them I needed some serious me time. They relented, but only after helping me up the stairs.

When I got to my room—blissfully solo now—I found it transformed. The place practically sparkled it was so clean. Clearly my mother had violated the large "DO NOT ENTER" sign on the door. I had an initial instinct to launch into a stomping tirade about personal privacy, but then I imagined her juggling a screaming Henry and numerous laundry bags while dusting and re-stacking videogames using her toes—kind of like that Octopus-handed bartender in *Who Framed Rodger Rabbit*. So, just this once, I figured I could let it slide.

Closing the door behind me, I went straight to my freshly made bed and collapsed. I stared up at the ceiling awhile, then reached for my iPad. It had Netflix on it, and more importantly, Netflix had *Firefly*. I needed it. I needed to escape. The frontier world of *Serenity* and Captain Reynolds and the Border Planets was such a better world than the one I was living in. People didn't die of horrible diseases there; they just had adventures. Sure, they had adversity, but they always overcame it. All the crew ever needed was wit, guile and a dash of luck, and everything could be solved. How was I supposed to do the same? Because if I were Captain Reynolds (although technically I'd be Kaylee), it'd be so much easier. I'd find some daring solution. I'd discover that there was a rare cure somewhere, and that the evil Alliance had it stowed away in a secret vault. Then I'd come up with a plan. It'd be daring and cool and fun. I'd break into the fortress and I'd beat up the guards. I'd encounter unexpected trouble and figure a way out. I'd snatch up the goods and I'd rocket away on my spaceship. Then, when everything was right with the world, I'd sit down with the crew in that rustic kitchen for supper and have some well-earned laughs.

Why can't *real life* be like that? Why does real life have to suck so much? Is it any wonder that when people say "in the *real* world," they're talking about something sucking? Because seriously, why is there stuff like cancer anyway? Whose bright idea was *that*? I mean, I guess people have to die of something, but still. At *fifteen*? Robbed of a future? How does that help anybody?

This was getting depressing. Definitely time for *Firefly*. I put on my favorite episode, entitled "Out of Gas." Now, of course *I* have seen it a hundred times, but just in case you're a crazy person and haven't, here's the plot: There's an accidental explosion in *Serenity's* engine room while the crew is in the kitchen celebrating the doctor's birthday. The blast knocks out the ship's life support and they can't fix it. Eventually—because they're running out of air—the crew has to abandon ship. All except the captain. He stays. Meanwhile, there are a bunch of flashbacks that explain how the various crewmembers came together in the first place. First officer, Zoe. Pilot, Wash. Mechanic, Kaylee. Tough guy, Jayne.

Anyway, about half way through, my eyelids started taking on a life of their own. The week's exhaustion had suddenly come over me like a warm blanket. My sleep at the hospital had been crappy at best, and there's nothing so nice as your own bed. I blinked to keep my eyes open. I was determined. I was going to see the episode through to the very end. It was *Firefly* after all. I was going to finish no matter wh—

"Figured I'd find you here," he said to me, my feet dangling off the catwalk above the cargo bay. My back was turned but I knew the voice.

"Hi Captain," I said.

He then asked if I was, "looking to be by my lonesome," which is just how he talks. I responded by scooting over. The grated metal walkway was a little rough on the butt, but it was still my favorite place to sit. It was like the ship's version of a front porch.

"Brought some tea." He handed me a warm tin cup as he took a seat, his legs dangling longer than mine.

I looked at him strangely and he smiled. "Didn't say it was for myself," he added. "Crew thought you'd like it."

"Thanks."

I took a sip and it was good. Kinda fruity. Then we sat together awhile, staring out over the empty hold. Well, not totally empty. There were a few odd crates and barrels, all tied down with ropes and webbing. There was the four-wheeled "mule," for hauling goods off the ship. There were boxes of foodstuffs for the kitchen. Technically, I suppose it wasn't much of a view. But as far as I was concerned, there wasn't a better one in all the Verse. On that point, I'm certain the captain would've agreed.

"It's so nice here," I finally said.

He let a long silence linger. "It's home," he finally said. "A home is always a pretty sight."

"Especially when it's a spaceship," I agreed.

He chuckled at that, and then fell silent again. He was waiting for me to say what was on my mind. It was one of his captainy tactics. I tried to just study my cup for as long as I could, but eventually I had to look up.

"Captain?" I asked.

"Hm?"

"Things are pretty rotten right now, sir."

I felt his gaze shift over to me, warming me. "I know it," he said gently.

"What do I do?"

He looked back out over the ship. The air was cool and quiet around us. "Not rightly sure," he answered. "Some things just have their course. Can't do much to change that. But sure as I know anything, bumpy rides end. Always do."

"Can't I just stay here?" I asked.

He shifted a little. "That might do ya for a spell, I suppose. But this boat's not your home. You got one of those already. And it's a long, long ways from here."

I took another sip and fell silent again. I knew he was right. He always was. And thoughts of Sid and Thu and my mom and dad and little Henry flit past me like a quick little carousal of faces. A sudden lump rose in my throat. My friends. My family. I loved them all so much. Each and every one of them—so different and yet so *mine*. They were my crew. At least, for now.

"Could be there's a place for you here," the captain added. "But that's what's comin', not what's now. You got some livin' to do first. I'd recommend gettin' to it."

I finally mustered the courage to look up at him—that familiar face, with its square jaw and twinkling eyes. I said, "I really do love your ship, Captain. I always have."

The corner of his mouth turned up slightly. It was like he'd remembered an old joke. "Ship's a pile of metal, darlin'. Just a big pile of parts. It's the folk inside that make her what she is."

"Still looks cool…" I offered.

"Well, I can't argue with that. Prettiest ship I ever saw. But you know what I like most?"

"What?"

"Those." He pointed to the hold's large double doors that exited the ship. "The comins and goins," he said. "Every time we set her down and every time we fly, we go through those doors together. Call it what you like—a team, a family, a crew—it all boils down to the same thing: we do for each other. Simple as that. Now don't go tellin' no one, but that's my favorite part."

"You mean it's not the harrowing getaways?"

"Absolutely not." He chuckled nervously. "Ain't no one enjoys those, just the moment right after. But for serious. It's the crew that matters, not the ship. Remember that."

"I will."

"Now I reckon it's time for you to wake up. There's yet work to be done, and there's only you to do it."

"Do I have to go now? Like, *right now?*"

He smiled and put a firm hand on my shoulder. "I'll be seein' you real soon, little Chloe. It's all right. Best you go on now."

With that, my eyes opened. It was barely dawn and blue grey light filtered through the window. My iPad was gone and my covers had been pulled up around me. My parents must have crept inside to tuck me in. I imagined them doing it, whispering and trying not to wake me. The thought filled me with a sudden warmth. They were such good people. I needed to do right by them—to "do for them" as Captain Reynolds had said. I needed to do as much as possible with whatever time I had left.

So then, at that very moment, I made a very, *very* important decision.

ONE HUNDRED FORTY-ONE DAYS

I'D DECIDED TO SIMPLY CALL IT, "The Plan." Not too creative, I know, but I needed to conserve my creativeness. The point was pretty simple. In fact, it was just basic arithmetic. The way I saw it, I loved my family and I loved my friends. But once I was gone, it would be like that love got subtracted. So it was easy. I just needed to add some more of it into their lives so that when the day came, it'd be like nothing happened. They wouldn't have to be sad. Cool, right?

Besides, this seemed like a far better idea than a "bucket list." I mean, really. If Heaven turns out to be a giant bowling alley where everyone just sits around talking about that one time they saw the Eiffel Tower or climbed Machu Picchu, I'm going to be very disappointed. Plus, most of *my* bucket list consisted of things involving castles, wizards, spaceships and lightsabers, so either way, I was plum out of luck.

So the question of the hour was: "How could I help?" For Thu and Dawson's Creek it was obvious—get them back together. That was item number one. Check.

What about Sid? What did he need? A GIRLFRIEND was the first thing that came to mind. But who? I needed to think about it.

Then there were my parents. Very tricky indeed. What could I possibly do for them? No matter what I did, they'd still be losing their daughter. (Which would suck pretty bad, I'm guessing.)

And little Henry… He was both easy and impossible at the same time. On the one hand, he was too small to know what was happening. On the other, I couldn't really communicate with him. I could literally give him a pony or a piece of tissue paper and he'd be equally happy with both. I'd have to think about this one as well.

So that's what I did. I spent the next hour brainstorming. By six, the muted sounds of Mom, Henry, and Woz's jingling collar floated past my door for their morning run. (I still didn't understand how that woman managed to juggle them all and still get in her exercise, *or* why she insisted on it.)

By seven, Chewbacca let me know it was time to get up. I hit the snooze, stared up at the ceiling a bit longer, and then finally dragged myself out of bed. I felt a lot better than the past few days, but that didn't change the fact that I wasn't a morning person. If I had my way, noon would be the universal starting point of all days across the globe. Nothing would be allowed to happen before then—absolutely nothing.

I headed downstairs, still wearing my clothes from yesterday. When I got to the kitchen, my parents were already laying out the table while Henry sucked on a bottle in his high chair. Woz was passed out cold.

"Morning, sweetheart," Mom called as I walked in. Whatever she was cooking smelled delicious. Omelets maybe?

"Morning," I said back, wafting over to Henry to give him a quick kiss. "What are you making?"

"Hash browns. But with sweet potatoes."

I smiled. Mom was a big, big fan of sweet potatoes, and a big, big hater of regular ones.

Dad moved beside me as he brought plates and kissed my cheek. "You were out like a light last night," he said.

"Yeah, sorry. I fell asleep watching a show."

He looked shocked. "Are you kidding? Don't apologize. After I stole your iPad, I watched the next two episodes of *Firefly* on it."

"Three episodes," Mom muttered, still concentrating on the frying pan. "Loudly."

Bright eyed, my dad continued, "Have you seen the 'Jaynestown' episode? I had no idea it was that good!"

I looked at him, incredulous. "Have *I* seen it? Dad, I have it memorized."

"Oh yeah? Then I guess you can sing the Jayne song?"

He was referring to the song written about the show's resident tough guy, Jayne Cobb, because the people of this small town mistook him for a folk hero. (You have to see the show to understand why this is so funny.)

"I could," I said. "But I'm not."

"*Jayne!*" my dad trilled in a suddenly horrible singing voice. "*The man they call Jayne!*"

I winced. "Dad, oh my god. Early? Morning?"

"*He robbed from the rich, and he Gave. To. The. Poor—* it's really quite catchy, you know?"

"Please…"

"*He stood up to the man, and he Gave. Him. What. For. Our love for him now ain't hard to explain. The hero of Canton, the Man. They. Call. Jayne!*"

"Honey," Mom interrupted sweetly. "If you keep singing that song I'm going to murder you." She brought a steaming stack of hash browns over to the table as she spoke.

"Mom, this looks incredible," I said, taking a square. I actually meant it too. Healthy and tasty seldom went hand in hand, but every once in a while…

"I second that," Dad echoed. "All we need now is some Mudder's Milk."

This was another Jaynestown reference and my mom glared at him. "Can you get Henry, please?" she said. (I'd come to learn that this meant "change his diaper before violence ensues.")

"On it," Dad replied with a salute.

I laughed. It was good to see them joking a bit. My parents really did love each other—it was obvious. But with so much everyday life—not to mention Everywhere Cancer—getting in the way, it was also obvious that they needed a boost. Sort of like another log on the fire, you know? So that was it. That's what I needed to get for them. I wasn't sure *how* just yet, but if there was one thing I had, it was a big imagination. And so, like the wild-haired wizardess that I am, I began stirring the glowing cauldron in my brain, letting out the odd cackle… and brewing stratagems.

ONE HUNDRED
FORTY DAYS

HERE'S ANOTHER CRUMBY THING about coming home from the hospital: jumping back into your life like nothing's happened. Only of course, something *has* happened, and by this point, every single person in school probably knows about it. It was all those awkward looks of sympathy/curiosity that sucked the most. It made me feel like a carnival attraction. I'd been through it before in middle school and now, guess what? I got to go through it again in high school!

It's a little understood fact that sympathy actually stings worse than meanness when you're sick. Or at least, it does when you're the type of sick that never gets better. All you want to do is feel normal, which is impossible when everyone is looking at you like, "*Oh my god, I'm so sorry!*"

But anyway. Tomorrow I had to go back to school. My stomach was literally doing hula-hoops around my waist. I tried reading, watching TV, and even looking at some piles of homework I'd missed; yet nothing worked. I needed a bigger distraction. I needed to *do* something.

I'd thought more about The Plan and had a good idea for Henry. Perhaps now was the best time to get started.

I ran downstairs and announced I was heading to the park. Hesitantly, my parents said okay, and the next thing I knew, I was pedaling The Pink Menace (the name of my bike, which is a long story unto itself) to my very favorite spot. I called it

Hiding Hill. There was this little public park a few blocks from my house, and in the middle of it was this low mound of earth with a sprinkling of trees on top. It was the world's most perfect place to sit, think, doodle in the dirt, and enjoy the quiet. This time, however, I had a mission. I found a shady patch beneath a tall elm, sat down, and got to it.

"Got to what," you ask?

Well, here's what I was going to do for Henry: I was going to write him a letter. Not an email or a tweet, but a bona fide, old school article of correspondence, like the type he'd keep for the rest of his life. And hand-written, too. That way a little piece of me would come with it. He'd look at the pen strokes—years from now—and think, "*Huh. Her actual hand did this...*"

It was a great idea. (And the only one I could think of.) All that was left now was to write it. I started out, as I often did, by making a list. It was entitled:

Things to Talk About in Henry's Letter.

Then, with my best swirly writing, a made a beautiful "1." at the top.

I stared at it. A minute passed. Then another. A few more. I tapped my pen. I looked around. Took my finger and doodled in the dirt...

I was in the middle of drawing a terrific pterodactyl/generic bird shape when a great *whoosh* distracted me. The gust of wind was so powerful it nearly knocked me over. I looked up to find a familiar sight. Dark green scales. Big reptilian eyes. Huge teeth. Its wings were twice as wide as a school bus. Somehow, I knew better than to be afraid though. I'd seen it so many times already, and so far, there hadn't been a single fire-breathing incident.

It settled at other end of the hilltop, coming to rest on all fours. It stared at me, all curious-like, with its head slightly cocked.

I stared back, dumbfounded.

Now, I know what you are thinking. You're thinking that this dragon isn't really real, right? Of course that's what you're thinking.

Well, all I can say is that it looked plenty real to me. I could see it. I could hear it. I could probably touch it too, but that didn't seem like a good idea.

Finally, feeling bold, I said, "Hello?"

It stared back, cocking its head even deeper.

"Are you a dream?" I asked.

Nothing.

"Are you ever going to leave me alone?"

Silence.

"Do you have a name?"

More silence.

"Fine," I said, suddenly resolute. "But if you're going to keep following me around, I'm giving you one."

It snorted like a giant horse, only—of course—there was a puff of fire involved.

"I'm calling you..." I said, then paused, looking down at my diary. The only thing written was still the title. "I'm calling you... *Hank,*" I said.

The dragon just stared. Then, as if deciding I was too small for a proper meal, he lay down, resting his giant head on the grass. He kept a wary eye on me, but mostly, he just looked sleepy.

Well, I thought. *I guess that's better than mad?*

So we sat together like that, both kind of ignoring the other. It was oddly peaceful. I got the feeling that with him around, there wasn't anything anywhere that could ever harm me. So long as he was there, I was safe. (Ironic, right?) And so I got to work on Henry's letter, thinking of nothing else.

ONE HUNDRED
THIRTY-NINE DAYS

APPARENTLY, ONE OF THE MOST famous quotes from Shakespeare is, *"All the world's a stage, and all the men and women merely players."*

I didn't really know what he meant by that, but on my first day back at school, I sure understood the whole "stage" part. Literally everyone was looking at me. Not *gawking*—just glancing in that way like they were trying not to. Which was worse.

When my mom dropped me off, Sid and Thu were already waiting. It felt like they were a pair of publicists shielding me from a crowd of paparazzi, only a.) no one was taking pictures, and b.) no one was crowding. Still, that's what it felt like.

I made it to my first few classes okay. English. Trig. History. Spanish. The teachers welcomed me back, but didn't make any big gestures about it. Mostly I just listened, took notes, and glanced at the clock. I remembered the differing second hands from my first day. English ticked. Trigonometry oozed.

Eventually it was lunch, and Sid and Thu intercepted me before I reached the quad. They clung to my arms, once again doing their human shield routine. Sid kept me entertained with stories of what I'd missed the previous week. Thu provided counterweights to his many embellishments.

I listened, but didn't say much. The truth was I felt awkward. I'd never liked being the center of attention, and I'd never had much practice either. Out in the quad, everyone at Brick Wall Place had their eye on me, even when they didn't. It was like I was wearing a giant, floppy hat or something.

Finally I just said completely out of the blue, "Hey, can we pretend like last week didn't happen?"

Everyone sort of stopped and stared for a second before Sid's face lit up. "I think I know what's needed here," he said briskly. "Watch this."

He reached into his lunch bag, grabbed a grape, and threw it so high it literally disappeared into the sky. Staring up, he ran in an awkward circle, tripped, somersaulted back to his feet, and then with great aplomb caught the grape in his mouth. He raised his arms in triumph, beaming with his patent, mega-smile.

"That was pitiful," Tad announced, hopping off the wall. "Let me show you how a professional does it."

And just like that, with a grape, Everywhere Cancer was gone. Everyone joined in on the contest. First it was just my friends. Then a crowd gathered. Freshmen, sophomores, juniors, seniors. Sid stayed in the middle of it—a king amidst a circle of spectators. They laughed, made bets, taunted.

I watched them from the edge, actually laughing for the first time since the hospital. I remembered my *Firefly* dream. Captain Reynolds and home and where you're meant to be. My crew was right here. Sid, Thu, Tad, Dawson's Creek. They were doing for me like I needed to do for them. No matter what, I couldn't fail. The Plan had to work.

I caught Sid's eye before he launched another grape. He smiled and a sudden lump rose in my throat. I couldn't help it.

Siddhartha Patel, I thought, watching him bend and throw with all his might. *I'm going to miss you.*

ONE HUNDRED THIRTY-FIVE DAYS

DR. MARK HAD ONE of those massive smart phones that could only fit in the pocket of a giant—which I suppose he was.

"Move the catapults over here," he said, pointing as I held the phone with both hands in his office. "If they attack you on the flanks, you'll be covered."

I nodded sagely. "Yes," I said.

"And upgrade the Barracks. You're going to need Mage Knights."

"I already have the Fire ones."

"Mages are better. Seventy HP."

"Okay."

I spent the remainder of my gold, lumber and iron on the upgrade. The game was called *Fortunes of Empire,* and it was one of those games where you build up a kingdom with castles, barracks, farms, etc, so you can create an army of warriors and go attack someone else's kingdom. I *adored* it.

"What do I do while it's upgrading?" I asked.

He peered at the screen a second. "Make more peasants. It's all about the resources."

I did.

"Now what?"

"Gotta wait. The game makers want you to spend money on Power Gems so you can play faster, but I urge patience. Just play a few minutes here and there throughout the day. You won't have to spend a dime."

"I'll download it," I said, staring fixedly at the screen. My kingdom was already a bustling metropolis after only a few minutes.

"You know what's cool?" he asked.

"What?"

"Well, maybe not 'cool,'" he mused. "But interesting?"

"What?"

"It's all just math."

I looked up. "Huh?"

He shrugged his basketball player shoulders. "It's just math," he repeated. "The code behind the game. Like, look at your swordsman there."

I tapped on one of the swordsmen and his stats popped up.

"See? He's got thirty Health and four Damage," Dr. Mark said, pointing.

"So?"

"So behind the screen he's just a little piece of code. When he 'fights,' he subtracts the number four from other little pieces of code. The other pieces, in turn, subtract numbers from him. Like the Mage Knight for example—who of course isn't really a Mage Knight. He's a little cartoon on top of an invisible number. But if the drawing weren't there, the game wouldn't be any fun. Get it?"

I scrunched my nose. Dr. Mark had clearly given this way too much thought. Talk about someone who needed a girlfriend...

"Sort of?" I said.

"That's all it is," he said triumphantly. "Just numbers adding and subtracting on a screen. The characters are only there so you'll care about it."

I stole my eyes away to squint at him crossly. "My swordsman is *not* a number. He's a mighty warrior."

He chuckled and put his hands up in surrender. "He is. Totally."

"I'm still downloading the game," I told him.

"You should. I play it every day."

"Between Power Rangers conventions?" I said.

"*Ouch.*" He put a fist to his chest like he'd been wounded. "A low blow!"

I stuck my tongue out at him.

He said, "So aside from *Fortunes of Empire,* are you sure you don't have any other questions?"

"The square root of 324?" I asked.

"Eighteen. Anything else?"

(He was obviously hinting at doctory type stuff now.)

"I'm good," I chirped. "But can I keep your phone?"

"No."

"Okay then. Same time next week?"

"Same time next week," he said. "I expect to see some serious *Empire* action by then. Lots of conquered lands."

I hopped off the exam table. "I'll be sure to do my math homework then."

He chuckled. "Very clever. And by the way, since we're all nerds here, type 'Plato' into Google and watch some of the YouTube videos that come up. That's where I got idea for the whole 'invisible math,' thing. You'll dig it."

I frowned at him. "Geez, Dr. Mark. You're getting pretty philosophical these days."

He shrugged again. "It's just a thought." He then pointed a long, accusatory finger at me. "And upgrade those Mage Knights as soon as you have the elixir. That's crucial."

• • •

On the drive home with my mom, I asked her, "Is Dr. Mark married?"

She looked at me askance. "I think he's a little old for you, sweetie."

Ugh.

First of all: *obviously.* Second of all: He's not *old* old. He's like in his thirties or something. And handsome.

"I'm just asking, like, *in general,*" I said.

She put her eyes back on the road, shifting in her seat. "Why do you ask?"

"I don't know," I said. "I just noticed he wasn't wearing a wedding ring or anything. And he's so cool. I wondered what his deal was."

She took a deep breath. It looked like she was about to say something, but couldn't find the words. Her mouth just sort of opened and closed for a minute. Eventually she said, "Are you really sure you want to know?"

Well *now* I did. Was I sure I wanted to know what?

"Uh... yeah?" I said.

She took another breath. "He... *was* married."

"Was?"

"His wife died in a car accident last year, honey. I only heard about it a couple weeks ago. Some of the moms were talking in the waiting room. I didn't know how to tell you."

ONE HUNDRED TWENTY-EIGHT DAYS

IF PLUTO SUDDENLY EXPLODED, it would take about four hours for anyone to see it. Crazy, right? An entire planet going *boom,* and for the length of a double feature, no one would be the wiser. I guess it's kind of like that with people too. Horrible things happen to them, but if no one tells you, it's like nothing ever happened.

It had been a week since Mom told me about Dr. Mark, and I still couldn't believe it. I felt awful—all this time and I hadn't even said I was sorry. I'd just babbled on and on about Power Rangers and how he was such a dork. He must have been in so much pain, and yet he never showed it. Not a single bit.

I was scheduled to see him after school today for another weekly checkup. I had no idea what to do or what to say. All I knew was that every fiber of my being wanted to run up and hug him like the giant redwood tree that he was.

But I knew I couldn't.

If Dr. Mark was anything like me, he was doing all he could to avoid thinking about it. Just press forward, shoulders up, like heading into a rainstorm.

"Chloe?" A kind voice interrupted my thoughts. "Are you all right, darling?"

It was Miss Collins, looking at me from the other side of the Drama room. I suddenly realized I'd been doing my patent "Stare Blankly at the Wall Whilst Thinking" routine.

"Fine," I squeaked, refocusing. The class was standing in a wide circle around the rehearsal stage. We did this at the beginning of every class for our horrendously embarrassing warm-up exercises—or as Miss Collins liked to call them, "our nuclear war on sheepishness." They generally involved some combination of singing, dancing and shouting. Sid, of course, was a natural.

"Right." Miss Collins moved into the middle of the circle. "We have a big day of rehearsals ahead, so we're going to supersize our dance party warm-ups. Therefore today—and today alone—I'm taking song requests. The first one to—"

"Straight Outta Compton!" Sid burst in a single syllable. It was like he'd been waiting to say the words his entire life.

Miss Collins turned to him, bemused. "Mr. Patel. While I appreciate your enthusiasm, I'm not sure if 'gangsta rap' is quite appropriate for a school setting. So if you don't mind, I think..." she suddenly paused, frowning. We all waited with bated breath. Finally, she sighed. "Oh very well," she said. "Let us '*play that shit,*' as one might say."

It was statements like that that earned Miss Collins a lot of points. She flipped through her phone a moment, plugged it into some speakers, and—well, you can probably imagine what the next few minutes looked like. Drama 1 became a rap video. And Sid... Sid could break dance like nobody's business. I had no idea.

Even Miss Collins joined in. The woman could *move* too. Like, really move. And when I saw that she—prim, English, and adorable—*knew the lyrics by heart...* I had a sudden and stupendous idea.

She was single.

Dr. Mark was single.

Oh yes. The Plan just got a little bigger.

ONE HUNDRED
TWENTY-FIVE DAYS

AT THIS MOMENT—if you've been paying attention—you might realize there's a big something that I've neglected to mention. I've been back at school for a full week now, and I haven't told you a single thing about ADAM WORLEY.

There's a good reason for this. But before we get to that, I wanted to amend some of my previous ramblings. It won't take long.

So remember when I first woke up in the hospital and ranted about that whole "teeth brushing" and "uncontrollable fate" thing? Well, I've realized that there's also an optimistic side to that. And here it is: Do you realize how much horrible stuff *doesn't* happen? Like, it could though, right? There could be car crashes all the time. People could trip and fall off bridges. Planes could fall out of the sky. A million things could go wrong every day. But they don't. Most of that stuff hardly ever happens at all.

So I guess my point is that when you really think about it, things go right a heck of a lot more than they go wrong. And I don't know about you, but that gives me a lot of hope.

Anyway, I only mention this because last week—regarding the Adam Worley situation—I got really, really lucky. Like, gift from Heaven lucky. Throughout the entire week, the boy had been blissfully absent from class. Why, you ask? Well, let's not dwell on that. Such reasons are unimportant. All that really matters is...

Okay, fine. He had the flu. And I'm a horrible person.

But oh my god, it was so awesome that he wasn't there. I couldn't even imagine how embarrassing it would have been if he was. It was as if the fates—or in my imagination the ancient Greek gods like Hermes and Zeus and stuff—finally got together and said, "You know what guys? Let's give her a break," and then zapped Adam Worley with the flu.

Am I awful for saying that? Probably. 'Tis in the judgment of the gods.

Today however—not so lucky.

Adam Worley was back, beautiful and spry as ever. And looking right at me. And saying things. And awaiting some form of verbal response.

I said, "Uh..." for a bit, kind of like singing a long dull note. I think his original question had been, "Are you feeling better?"

"Yeah," I finally said, gulping. "I mean, yeah, like breathtakingly. Breathtakingly better."

Time sort of slowed after I said that. I thought: *Breathtakingly? Twice?*

I watched in horror as the corner of Adam's lip turned up in amusement. "That's a... powerful adjective." He then smiled fully, adding, "And I'd have to say I agree. A hundred percent."

"Ha ha," I answered weirdly. And no, that doesn't mean I laughed. It means I literally said, "ha" and "ha," back to back. To recover, I quickly added, "Thanks."

He shrugged. "It's true. You look great." He leaned a little closer. "I'd use the word 'breathtaking,' but... might come across as a little creepy."

"Yeah," I said again, letting out an awkward laugh. "And..." I paused, brushing a stray curl behind my ear.

"What?" he asked.

"I just, um, wanted to say thanks, too. I mean, for helping me that night."

Before he could answer, the bell rang and Mr. Bowen jumped in front of the class. "Who knows what *entropy* is?!" he exclaimed.

Adam winked before turning his attention to our crazy teacher. I followed his gaze and saw that—predictably—no one had raised their hand. I guess I sort of knew what entropy was, but, well… Adam Worley was sitting next to me. And did he just *wink* at me?!

"Not to worry!" Mr. Bowen went on. "This muffin and this blowtorch,"—he held them aloft—"will teach us!"

I listened dumbly as Mr. Bowen explained about matter constantly moving toward states of greater disorder, but in my head all I could hear was: *DoesAdamWorleylikeme? DoesAdamWorleylikeme?   DoesAdamWorleylikeme? DoesAdamWorleylikeme? DoesAdamWorleylikeme?*

I mean, he might, right? He said I looked great/breathtaking. He winked when I thanked him. And… well, that was about it, but still!

I beamed.

I sat straighter.

I glowed.

And Mr. Bowen charbroiled a muffin with a blowtorch.

ONE HUNDRED
TWENTY-TWO DAYS

A FEW DAYS LATER, I made a quick mental recap of the targets for The Plan. They were as follows:

1. Dawson's Creek and Thu Pham. I would bring these star-crossed lovers back together.... no matter how much they hated each other. Or *pretended* to. It was true love, and everyone knew it.

2. Siddhartha Patel. My best friend was going to get his first real girlfriend, and I knew exactly who that girl needed to be. Emily Sulecki—the impossibly hot girl who no one thought he had a chance with. I, however, knew better.

3. Dr. Mark and Miss Collins. The more I thought about it, these two were made for each other. All I needed to do was get them in a room together and it would be love at first sight.

4. Mom and Dad. These two used to be the biggest cheeseballs when I was growing up—always flirting and poking fun at each other. They needed to be that way again. Even after I was gone.

5. Henry Cartwright. My little brother was going to grow up to be awesome, I just knew it. I could see it in his eyes. And I'd be darned if I couldn't claim some of the credit. His big sister was going to give him the best advice ever.

So that was it. Five separate missions. They would require planning and ingeniousness. Luckily, I happened to be an expert in both. It was time to get to work. Right away. Posthaste. And as a side note: can one be an expert in "ingeniousness?" I didn't know. But I was going to find out.

ONE HUNDRED
TEN DAYS

A COUPLE WEEKS LATER, I pedaled The Pink Menace over to Sid's house after dinner. (Kale and spinach salad with butternut squash chunks and Greek yogurt dressing. If I could make a barfing sound right now, I would.)

I'd always enjoyed a "No Knocking Necessary" policy at the Patel's so I let myself in without ringing the bell. I was about to head upstairs when I heard what sounded like an argument coming from the living room. Cautiously, I crept forward, tiptoeing on the wood flooring. My plan was to peek around the corner, determine if I was interrupting some sort of family squabble, and then stealthily return outside and pedal away.

I managed to accomplish step one of that plan, only to get caught a second later.

"Baffling, isn't it?" Sid said, making me jump. He was lounging at his kitchen table and eating a bowl of popcorn.

"Sorry," I said quickly. "I just…" I paused, looking at the odd scene in the next room. "What are they *doing?*" I asked.

Sid gestured for me to come sit. "Welcome to my life," he said wryly.

Mr. and Mrs. Patel were locked in what seemed to be an epic contest of wills; only they weren't speaking English. They were using some form of alien code. Behind them, as they argued, stood a large chalkboard covered in strange symbols and incomprehensible writing.

It took me a second to put two and two together (no pun intended for the upcoming explanation), but I once again remembered Sid's greatest hardship in life: he wasn't a genius.

Sure, he was plenty smart, but he wasn't a bona fide genius. For most people, this wouldn't be a problem, but for him it was different. He was a member of the Patel family.

Every single one of the Patels was like a Nobel Prize winner. His dad was this ultra programming bigwig at Google—and from his wild, Einsteinian hairstyle—I imagined he was the guy working on the real life version of Skynet. His mom was a mathematics professor at Stanford and—according to Sid—an occasional Top Secret consultant for the government. His older brother—at nineteen— was a junior at MIT. And his little sister, Piya, whom I adored, was only eleven and already the captain of our school's Mathletes team, The Denominators. (She'd skipped a few grades.) Altogether, the Patel's were a serious mathematical force. All except Sid. He got a B- in Algebra 2 last year.

"I believe they call it 'combinatory mathematics,'" he explained, taking another handful of popcorn.

Absently, I took some for myself. "Do they do this every night?"

"No." He shook his head. "I think this is their version of 'date night.' They wheel out the old chalkboard, start writing obscure equations on it, and then argue their heads off. They love it."

"That's kind of romantic, actually."

Sid looked at me. "Oh yeah. They're a regular Wesley and Buttercup."

"I *love* that movie," I said breathlessly, taking another handful of popcorn. I thoroughly enjoyed watching the Patels.

It was like they were in their own little world. They hadn't even noticed me yet.

Sid suddenly sat straighter and put on a serious face. "*Hello,*" he said solemnly. "*My name is Inigo Montoya. You killed my father. Prepare to die.*"

Without thinking, I responded, "*I only dog paddle.*" (One of my most obscure talents was doing a near perfect impression of Andre the Giant from *The Princess Bride*. Everyone knew it.)

Sid laughed. "I knew I could get you to do that."

"When you've got it, flaunt it," I said airily. "Speaking of which, I'm going to need your help."

"With what?"

"A secret mission of utmost importance."

"I'm in."

"I've brought schematics and plans."

He stood, pushing aside the popcorn. "Let's go."

We headed up the stairs to his room. Outside his door, however, stood a girl even shorter than me with her arms tightly crossed.

"Out of the way, midget," Sid ordered, but her eyes only narrowed.

"You're not supposed to call me that," she snapped, then added brightly, "Hi Chloe!"

"Hey Piya," I said.

She smiled and then quickly went back to scowling at her big brother. "You stole my computer again, perv face. And your stupid door is locked."

"First of all, it isn't *your* computer. Second of all—"

"It has my name on it!" she squeaked. "And just because you broke yours looking at dirty pictures doesn't mean—"

"That is *so* not what happened! I was just—"

"Give it back!"

"What do you need it for, anyway?" Sid asked, shoving her aside and getting out his keys. The actual *keys* weren't what he was after, though. What he needed was the keychain. It was a heavy electromagnet. He pressed it to the upper part of the door (which Piya couldn't reach) and slid it sideways undoing the latch on the other side. Basically, he'd found a loophole to his parents' "no locks" policy by arguing, "No key? No lock."

"Homework," Piya said.

Sid opened the door and we went in. An alarm system barked, "*Intruder!*" before he switched it off.

Piya instantly ran past him and plopped herself on his bed. "So what are you guys up to?" she asked merrily.

Sid unplugged her computer and starting winding up the cord. "Nothing that concerns you, toadstool." He handed it over. "Now scram."

"I could help," she offered.

"No."

"Yes!" I piped up, sitting next to her.

She beamed at me and then at him, triumphantly.

Sid gave me a pleading look. "Please, no," he said.

"She's going to be our scribe," I answered.

Without hesitation, Piya opened her laptop and made ready to type. Her eyes were wide as saucers as she looked between the two of us.

"See?"

"But she's a little barf puddle," Sid complained.

"Am not!"

"She's not a 'barf puddle,'" I said. "And seriously, how old are you? We can trust her. Besides, she's smarter than the both of us."

Piya beamed even brighter. "That's right," she said. "Piya can be trusted and she's smarter than you." She stuck her tongue out at him for emphasis.

Sid sighed resignedly. "Whatever," he said, plunking himself down at his desk. "So what's this secret project of yours?"

I scooted up on the bed to sit cross-legged and swung my backpack into my lap. "Okay," I said, taking out my notebook. "I'm still working out the details, but for now, I'm calling it The Plan."

ONE HUNDRED EIGHT DAYS

OBVIOUSLY, I TOLD SID I had something in store for him as well, but he couldn't know what it was. He complained for an hour or two but eventually I convinced him that I needed to complete that part solo. So now, with Sid completely unawares, it was time to get operation Get Sid a Girlfriend v underway.

You see, you can learn a lot from movies. Especially if those movies are based on something by Shakespeare. If you recall, I mentioned earlier the movie, "Much Ado About Nothing," by Joss Whedon. It's one of my all time favorites, and also, it just so happens to contain a perfect recipe for love. The ingredients are very simple. All you do is take two people, tell each one separately that the other has a crush on them, get them alone together, and then stand back and watch the sparks fly. That's literally all it takes.

Anyway, we were all in Drama class, positioned around the stage for an off-book rehearsal of *Zombie Apocalypse*. (For most of us, including me, this was exceptionally easy since our only lines were "*Arragharghh!*" and other zombie type noises.) For Sid and his future girlfriend, however, there were lots and lots of lines. In the script, neither of them had names—just "Guy" and "Girl." They were currently in the middle of performing Act I, Scene 2, in which they have just arrived at a fancy Italian restaurant, only to find it deserted. (Because everyone's a zombie.)

GUY: Well, this is weird.

GIRL: Should we go somewhere else?

GUY: But the reviews… Let's check the kitchen.

GIRL: Hold on. I have to Snap this. It's so weird, right?

GUY: Definitely snap worthy.

GIRL: I know.

GUY: Hey, check this out!

GIRL: What?

GUY: The kitchen's empty but there are all these entrées prepared.

GIRL: Like recently?

GUY: Looks like it.

GIRL: Wait. Did you set this up? To be romantic???

GUY: Would you like me better if I said yes?

GIRL: I… uh… *crap!* I forgot my line again, Miss Collins.

GUY: Oh, come on! It's "*I think I'd LOVE you better!*" Seriously, how many times are you going to screw it up?

GIRL: Shut up!

GUY: I'm just saying.

GIRL: We can't all be obsessed with drama, okay! And you know what? Your face looks weird!

MISS COLLINS: Whoa. Let's all take a five-minute break, shall we?

GUY: Fine!

GIRL: FINE!

Sid and Emily both retreated to opposite corners of the room. Now, ordinarily, I would've gone to sit with Sid, but this was my chance. I walked over to Emily. Her long red hair was draped over her face as she hunkered over a copy of the script, rereading it furiously.

"Sorry about Sid," I said, sitting next to her.

She looked up with bright cheeks. "How can you *stand* that guy?"

"Years of practice." I smirked. "He's actually really cool though, I promise. He just has a big head right now because he heard that *supposedly* April Gallagher likes him."

"*What?*"

I smiled inwardly. April Gallagher was like the all-star super girl for the senior class. She was one of those people who had it all—beauty, brains, volleyball scholarship to Dartmouth...

"Yeah," I said. "I couldn't believe it either, but apparently it's true. She thinks he's funny or something."

Emily looked disgusted. "Well, apparently she's out of her mind. He's the most annoying guy on the planet."

"Oh, believe me, I know. But actually—" I then paused, scrunching up my face.

"What?"

I looked at her a moment. "He'd kill me if I told you this."

"Told me what?"

I checked to make sure no one was listening. (Very dramatically.) "I actually have a theory of my own. He totally likes someone else."

"That makes no sense at all. But who?"

"Promise you won't say anything?"

She gave me a look. "I've got better things to do than gossip about Siddhartha Patel."

I took a breath. This was a crucial moment. I needed to somehow make her believe that Sid had a crush on her without making it seem weird or like I was his messenger. Basically, I needed to not freak her out.

"It's just," I began hesitantly. "I've seen him like this before. He always gets really defensive and mean when he likes someone."

"So?"

"So," I said, "I can't help but notice he's acting like a total idiot towards... *you*."

Emily blinked. "Wait, what? You don't mean? No. No, *gross!*"

I shrugged. "I can't be sure or anything, but I'd bet on it."

"Okay, stop. This is way too creepy to even think about and I have to memorize this."

"Well," I said casually. "Don't say I didn't warn you."

A few seconds later, Miss Collins called everyone back to rehearsals. Emily managed to get through the entire scene without missing any lines and Sid did the same. There was also—probably only noticeable to me—this awkward little spark between them now. It was like they hated each other, but also something else, too.

Once we were out in the halls after class, Sid sidled up to me, frowning. "What were you talking to that evil wench about?"

"Huh?" I asked innocently.

"Emily. I didn't think you knew her."

"I don't. Not really."

"Then what were you talking to her about?"

"I went over to apologize for you being such a jerk."

He gaped. "*Me a jerk?* She said my face looks weird!"

Your face does look weird, I thought.

"Well, what did she say?" he asked.

"About what?"

"When you apologized."

"Nothing."

"She said nothing? Like she just stared at you?"

I groaned and rolled my eyes. (Again, very dramatically.)

"What?" he said.

"You really are clueless, aren't you?"

"What are you talking about?"

"Nothing."

"Dude, don't be like that. I agreed to help you with your plan, didn't I? What is it?"

I wheeled on him sharply. "God, why are boys so *stupid?*" I screeched. "Is it like some universal decree that none of you can even tie your own shoes?"

"Uh…"

"She *likes* you, dummy! It's so obvious!"

I promptly stomped off, leaving him standing there flabbergasted. I honestly would've given anything to turn around and see the look on his face, but I had to keep up the charade. Once I was safely around the corner however—and confident he wasn't going to catch up—I allowed a giant, self-satisfied grin to creep across my face. I couldn't help it. My cheeks were literally glowing like some kind of cupid-inspired superhero.

I just totally DID THAT! I thought, giving a little fist pump. *I just Much Adoed About Nothing the crap out of those two lovebirds!*

ONE HUNDRED
THREE DAYS

AFTER SEVEN DAYS, five intensive planning sessions, and countless "are you *sure* Emily likes me?" questions, Sid and I had ironed out all the details of The Plan. It was a thing of beauty. Piya had taken copious notes. Tad Prescott had agreed to take part. Tools had been purchased. A date had been set.

Now all that was left was the waiting and the preparing. I still had a million things to do, which in no particular order included: learning to cook, mastering iMovie on my computer, bribing the owner of a tiny theater in San Francisco, and finally coming up with something to write in Henry's letter.

The good news was that I had a full month to accomplish these things. The bad news was... well, the *waiting*. Time was short, and I didn't like the idea of putting off The Plan for so long. But it couldn't be helped. Friday, November 6th, was the one day when all the stars aligned and every item on the list could be ticked off in a single moment of awesomeness. Sid insisted we call it D-Day, like the World War II day. I explained to him that that didn't make any sense and was a horrible analogy, but he insisted on it. "Military precision!" he kept shouting. So, D-Day it was. (He would also refer to it occasionally as Zero Hour, which got me even more confused.)

Anyway. I had a month to prepare. iMovie wouldn't be too hard. I had plenty of leftover birthday money for bribes.

And cooking… well, when it came to that, I would have to trust in the old saying that, "It's the thought that counts."

Henry's letter on the other hand—that thing actually had to be good and it wasn't going to write itself.

I pedaled over to Hiding Hill with my diary and once again stared at the blank pages. Hank, of course, was already waiting for me. (This seemed to be his favorite spot now.) His wings were spread wide as he lay lazily in the grass. I said hello to him, but like usual, he just eyed me without raising his head. If I didn't know any better, I'd say he looked seriously bored. Or maybe that's just how dragons look all the time? Who knows.

• • •

And so the weeks crawled by.

The weather got colder with more grey skies than blue, and the air got as crisp as an autumn leaf. I went to school, hung out with Sid and Thu, worked on The Plan, and made frequent visits to Hiding Hill. That last activity was for two purposes: 1.) Working on Henry's letter, and 2.) Getting out of the house.

The truth was that things were getting a little rocky between the parental units. The stress of everything was clearly getting to them. They were arguing more than usual—which was okay, I guess, but they weren't making up afterwards. That's the most crucial part. They only fought when they thought I couldn't hear, but, of course, I could. (Rule #1 to all the parents out there: Your kids can *always* hear. Closed doors accomplish nothing.)

I also managed to tune out a lot of this fighting with excessive amounts of YouTube. I hadn't forgotten about Mr. Bowen's assignment for a "Fun Final," and after considerable research, I'd decided my presentation would focus on quantum physics.

Now, before you say, "that sounds a little intense," just remember that I'm an expert in ingeniousness. Besides, the professor guy in the video explained it really well. Basically, he talked about how tiny things behave by a different set of rules than big things. And by tiny, I mean super tiny things like atoms and electrons. One of the coolest things he mentioned was that tiny particles can be in two places at once.

Think about that. Two places *at once*. Not just zipping back and forth really fast, and not just two things that look totally identical. One thing. Two places. Same time. To put that in *Firefly* speak, "That don't make no kinda sense!"

But, apparently, it does, and they do.

Anyway. I thought it was cool.

SEVENTY-THREE DAYS

FOUR WEEKS LATER and the day was here! Everything was set! Everything was ready! None of my targets, including Sid, had any idea what was coming! Also, I was getting ahead of myself!

D-Day was actually tomorrow. But it *felt* like today. The Plan was going into effect within 24 hours, so that sort of made it today, right? I mean, who cares what the calendar says? The whole concept of "today" is a totally abstract concept. The important thing is that love was in the air and lives were about to change. And I, I was to be the author.

SEVENTY-TWO DAYS

OKAY NOW IT REALLY WAS D-Day and I was literally shaking. I mean, crap. I knew I'd be excited about it and everything, but I didn't think I'd be like this. My *teeth* were chattering.

But there was no time to think about nervousness now. A metric ton of things needed preparing and coordinating. Speaking of which...

"This operation must be completed by oh four hundred," I remarked importantly as Sid started Vera. It took him a few tries, but eventually he got the old girl purring. (Albeit in a scary, I'm-about-to-explode kind of way.)

"You're using that wrong," he said, looking over his shoulder as he backed out of the school parking lot.

"Oh four hundred? No I'm not."

"I believe what you're looking for is *sixteen* hundred. Four hundred implies four in the morning."

I frowned as I mulled this over a moment. Was *this* why I was always so disoriented during every stupid war film? I'd always just figured they were movie mistakes...

I promptly stuck my nose in the air. "Well, of course *I* knew that," I said. "I just didn't think *you* did."

"I see. Well either way, by 4:00 a.m., everything will be taken care of."

I stuck my tongue out at him, but annoyingly, I don't think he saw it.

We arrived at Whole Foods a few minutes later. I handed Sid a copy of the shopping list. "Remember," I told him.

"Items twelve through twenty-three are yours. And get two of everything. There's no room for error."

He saluted. "Aye, Captain."

I suddenly got a creeping suspicion that today was going to be replete with military-speak. After all, we were calling it "D-Day." So stupid…

"Good," I said, and the shopping commenced.

Now here's the thing about me and shopping: I hate it. Although technically, there are a few things for which I enjoy shopping. Vintage t-shirts. Star Trek memorabilia. Halloween costumes. But *food* shopping is definitely not one of these things. Still, I had a detailed list, and all I needed to do was follow it.

Item One:

Gluten Free Wheat Flour—Two Sacks.

I scanned the signs above the isles and found my target. I ran to it. There was no time to waste. Once all these ingredients were purchased, there was still the adventure of turning it into something that semi-resembled the beautiful picture on the cooking website.

Item Two:

Jumbo Variety Bag of Organic Peppers

I suddenly realized it would've been smarter to list these ingredients by proximity to each other. No time to dwell, though. Off to the veggies. I waved to Sid as he wheeled by, riding on the back of his shopping cart. He was heading to Dairy. Goat cheese, no doubt.

Anyway, now's probably a good time to explain why we were buying all these things. But before we get to that, let's give you a refresher on The Plan. It consisted of the following five items:

1. Get Thu and Dawson's Creek back together.

2. Find Sid a girlfriend.

3. Fix up Dr. Mark and Miss Collins

4. Repair Mom and Dad's relationship

5. Write an awesome letter to baby bro.

So our current shopping spree was in service to Task #4. I had two things in store for my parents tonight. First, when they got home they were going to find a dining room transformed into an uber romantic getaway with candles and soft lighting and music and two piping hot pizza pies loaded with organic veggies. (Why pizza, you ask? Well, like all fitness fanatics, my mother has a borderline obsession with cheat meal pizza as being perhaps the most glorious thing planet Earth has ever offered to human beings.) The second thing they were going to find was a superbly edited video collage of old home movies that I'd secretly pilfered from my dad's computer these past few weeks. It was quite an amazing film. A perfect blend of seminal moments alongside candid instances of goofiness. If that didn't remind them both of what life was all about, then I didn't know what would.

Also, by they time they both got home; they were going to find the house blissfully empty. Henry would be in the midst of enjoying an extended stay with the Patelleros (the family that alternated days with my parents for daycare), and I would be at Sid's house, secretly carrying out Task #2.

I looked back down at my list.

Item 3:

Organic Extra Virgin Olive Oil

Yep. Definitely should've listed these better. I checked my phone. It was fifteen oh nine. (3:09 for the layperson.) I needed to hurry up. I'd previously estimated at least an hour to prepare all this stuff.

"Chloe, look!" Sid's voice came from behind.

I glanced up to see him gliding past me on his cart with a bundle of bananas balanced on his head.

"You're a weirdo!" I shouted after him, smiling.

Oh yeah. We were making soy ice cream banana splits, too.

· · ·

Three hours and twenty-two minutes later, everything was finally prepared. (An hour! Ha!) The dinning room had been fully transformed, the pizzas were waiting in the oven, and the desserts were keeping cool in the freezer. My dad usually got home around seven, so I'd left a note for him to make the last few preparations before Mom arrived at eight. (All he needed to do was turn on the oven and remember to take the pizzas out, so hopefully he could handle that.)

Anyway, I needed to ride over to Sid's house in a few minutes, but first, I headed up to my room, a.k.a. Mission Control. My desk was neatly organized with laptop, iPhone, notepad, pen, and granola bar.

Currently, Sid was overseeing the details of Operation Thu and Dawson's Creek from Remote Location Alpha. He was waiting in his car, presumably with a pair of binoculars, on the other side of the street from the Punjab Café, an Indian restaurant (obviously) owned by his aunt and uncle. Typically, said restaurant would be buzzing with costumers by now, but tonight it was completely empty due to a sign reading, "Closed for Special Event! Come Back Tomorrow!"

According to Sid, he was going to need to cover a thousand and one dishwashing shifts for his cousin, Ameet, for setting this up.

Basically, the task was pretty simple. Sid had sent separate texts to both Thu and Dawson's Creek, saying that his family was having an important party at the restaurant and attendance was mandatory. I even texted them as well, casually asking, "*U coming to Sid's thing?*" in case either of them thought something fishy was afoot. Apparently, neither did, and both agreed to come. Once the two lovers arrived, Sid would lock the front and back exits with the Café's remote-controlled alarm system. Lastly, a buffet of fresh entrees—thanks to Ameet—was already prepared and waiting. Guess where I got *that* idea from? (I'll give you a hint: it starts with "Zombie" and ends with "pocalypse .")

So. Thu and Dawson's Creek were about to have no choice but to sit down and have a romantic date together. And hopefully—after avoiding the spicier foods— start making out.

My phone buzzed with the Empire theme from *Star Wars*. I answered, and Sid's grinning visage appeared on the screen. The image bounced around as he walked. "Thu just arrived," he reported in a hushed tone. "And Dawson's Creek just texted. He's gonna be a couple minutes late."

"*Of course he is,*" I sighed, looking at my clock for the thousandth time. It was 6:37. "He's cutting it close." It then occurred to me that Sid wasn't inside his car like he should've been. I narrowed my eyes at him. "Why aren't you in Vera? What if they see you?"

He checked his surroundings again before glancing back at the phone. "No chance," he said firmly. "I'm a creature of the night."

"But—"

"Also," he added, "There's a problem with the remote thingy. It won't work from so far away."

"You said you tested it!"

"That was a half-truth. Ameet promised it would work and I believed him. But don't worry. It'll work now."

I groaned as I looked at the clock again. 6:38. Sweat was actually started to drip down my forehead. Months of ingenious planning were all resting on a few stray minutes of precision timing, not to mention a handful of unwitting pawns who had no idea they were playing staring roles in my grand scheme.

"Crap," Sid whispered suddenly. My eyes shot back to the screen and the video started thrashing about as he ran.

Horror-struck, I asked him what was happening.

"Dawson's Creek just pulled up. I don't think he saw me."

"Where are you now?"

"A bush. Don't worry. He's parking."

I waited in silence, not breathing.

"Okay, he's getting out now. He's... yes! He's heading to the restaurant. My god, he's dressed like an idiot."

The phone jostled again and I saw a distant, grainy image of Dawson's Creek walking across the parking lot. It kind of looked like that classic Bigfoot video where he's caught trudging through the woods.

"What's up with that jacket?" Sid said off screen. "It looks like something from *Back to the Future.*"

I laughed, but quickly stopped. "It doesn't matter. Just press the remote as soon as he's through the door. When he sees her, he might try to flee."

"I'm on it," he answered. "He should reach the door in about five, four, three, two... he's in!"

"Lock it!"

Several horrible seconds of silence passed before the image on the screen flipped around to show Sid's triumphant grin. "It's done," he announced.

"They're locked in?"

"Yep. I'm going back to Vera. Call you in a sec."

"You're awesome!" I quickly said before the video cut out.

I slumped back and checked the clock again. 6:43. Operation Thu and Dawson's Creek was underway. And on second thought, I totally should have bugged the restaurant. I could only imagine what they'd be saying to each other. Instead, I had to settle for the next best thing. The Punjab Café had two large windows in front, so Sid, with his binoculars, could see almost everything inside. His job was to make sure Thu and Dawson's Creek were peacefully sitting together before hastily returning to Casa de Patel. He needed to be there so that my cover story of "Studying at Sid's House Tonight" would hold up later on.

Next up was Tad Prescott. He and his new girlfriend Jen were in charge of Task #3—fixing up Dr. Mark and Miss Collins. This was the trickiest item of all. To sum it up, Miss Collins was performing a comedy show at this tiny theater in downtown San Francisco. The place could only hold like two dozen people, so—after speaking with the owner—I used up all my savings and bought up every single ticket in advance. Then, during one of my visits with Dr. Mark, I made a devilishly sly bet with him. I bet him that if I reached a certain level on *Fortunes of Empire,* then he'd have to do whatever I said. Naturally, I won this bet, and then handed him a single ticket for Miss Collins' play. He was confused by this, but I told him that it was super important to me that he went, and for emphasis, I gave him his ticket with a little Power Ranger attached. (It wasn't one of his rare collectables or anything, just a cheap one.)

However, it was now 6:45 and the play started at seven. Tad hadn't called yet, which meant Dr. Mark hadn't arrived, and if he didn't arrive soon, the entire plan would be ruined.

"Come on." I tapped my fingers anxiously as Tad's phone continued to ring. After a disconcerting *six* rings, Tad finally answered with a laugh, "Hey Chloe."

"Is he there?" I asked, skipping the hellos.

"Sorry," he answered. "I haven't seen anyone. There's still like twenty minutes though, right?"

I glanced at the clock. "Fourteen," I said. "But still. He *should* be there by now."

"I'm sure he'll show up."

I furrowed my brow a moment as I wondered what was taking him so long. Maybe there was traffic? Or a problem with parking? He hadn't gotten abducted by Jawas, had he?

I refocused on my phone as I heard what sounded like the muffled laughter of an impromptu wrestling match on the other end.

"Don't worry, Chloe," Tad said again. "I'm sure he'll show up."

I raised my chin in an effort to sound confident. "I know," I said. "Just call me when he does. And thanks, by the way. I seriously owe you."

"Ha! Are you kidding? I'm having the best date of my life!"

"*Awww,*" Jen's voice came over the line.

"Hey Jen!" I said loudly.

"*Hey!*"

"Okay, so just call me when he shows up."

"Will do," Tad answered distractedly. "Bye!"

Before I could say anything more the phone went blank.

Well, at least he's having fun, I thought, once again glancing at the clock. 6:49. This was now getting *waaaaay* too close. I needed to be out of the house in like two minutes. Dad would be home at seven, and while it wouldn't *totally* ruin the surprise if I were still here, it would still kinda suck. Plus, there was a chance he'd tell me I had to stay, and I wanted this night to be just the two of them.

Right then, Sid called, informing me that we might have a problem.

"What?" I asked.

"They don't look very happy."

"You mean like they're not talking?"

He gave a weak laugh. "Oh no, they're talking all right. Just... not in the friendliest of ways."

At this point I would've asked him to show me, but the view would've been way too far away. I had to rely on Sid's descriptive skills.

"What are they doing?" I asked.

"Well, they keep waving their arms and making threatening gestures."

Not necessarily bad, I thought. *Perhaps this was just a display of unbridled passion? I mean, that's what they say, isn't it? Love and loathing are almost identical at times?*

"Does it look they might start kissing?" I asked.

"I'd have to go with a 'negative' on that one, Commander."

"But what if—?"

"*Whoa!*" Sid cut me off. "Thu's trying to kick the door open!"

"*What?*"

"If she breaks it, Ameet's going to kill m—" his voice suddenly dropped to a low whisper. "*Oh no,*" he breathed. "I've gotta stop this."

I screeched, "Stop what?"

"She just picked up one of the chairs. I think she intends to break the glass with it..."

At that, Sid's phone fell from his hand in a chaotic rush of static and flipping video. It settled on Vera's floor, staring fixedly up at the ceiling from an awkward angle. After that, all I could hear were his quieting footfalls as he ran toward the restaurant.

In shock, I slowly reached over and hung up. I sat in complete silence, staring at the phone. I mean, I thought Thu and Dawson's Creek might be a little awkward at first, but *throwing chairs?*

My heart literally sank to my stomach. *And where the heck was Dr. Mark?* It was—I checked the clock—6:56!

Frantically, I redialed Tad.

"Hey Chloe," he said with a touch more worry this time. "He, uh, kinda hasn't shown up yet."

Okay, wow. Seriously? How could Dr. Mark do this? He *said* he'd be there. He promised. I gave him a Power Ranger!

"You're positive?" I asked desperately. "There's no chance you missed him?"

"Jen just peeked inside the theater. It's still totally empty."

Great, I thought. *Now Miss Collins won't have any audience at all!*

My throat tightened as I fought a sudden urge to cry. I had to salvage something from this.

I swallowed to keep my voice steady. "Okay," I said. "Do you and Jen both have your emergency tickets?"

Tad paused for a short, yet noticeable, second. "Uh, we do. Do you want us to go in?"

"Is that okay?" I asked. "Did you guys have other plans?"

"No, not at all," he said quickly. (He most definitely *did* have other plans, I could totally tell.) "We were just gonna walk around," he added brightly. "Besides, what could be a better date than a theater all to ourselves?"

I literally had to bite my lip to keep my voice from wavering. Now I had *three* things to feel guilty about. "The play's only an hour," I told him quickly. "And I totally owe you. And tell Jen I'm sorry. I really, really am. And please, please, please text me if he shows up."

"Will do," Tad said. "By the way, how are Thu and Dawson's Creek doing? Has Sid called you?"

My heart dropped even lower at the reminder. "I'm not sure," I lied. "Sid just told me they were both at the restaurant now."

"I'm sure they're doing great," Tad said. "You did a good thing there, Chloe. Seriously. I'll text you as soon as your doctor comes in. I'm sure he will."

"Me too. Thanks, Tad."

After hanging up, I once again stared blankly at my phone. No Dr. Mark. Thu and Dawson's Creek were kaput. Sid had run after them and dropped his phone. In some ways, that was the biggest disaster of all. It meant I had no way of calling him, and that my plans for him and Emily were in serious jeopardy. If he wasn't back at his house soon—

I jumped suddenly as my phone buzzed with a text. My heart leapt at the thought of it being Tad. *I knew Dr. Mark would show up!*

Then I read it.

DAD: Hi sweetheart. I'm sorry but there's an emergency at work and I have to stay late. I've already called the Patellero's so don't worry about Henry. I've also texted your mom, but she's probably with a client. If you see her, let her know I'll be home as soon as I can. Again, so sorry.

Love, Dad

Huh. Well then, Universe. What other plans would you care to ruin today? Perhaps a wedding? Or a birthday? I mean, it's not like you're not already on a roll...

I blinked at my phone numbly. It was like I'd just spent months building a giant, amazing sandcastle only to have a single wave come along and wipe it away into nothing. Dr. Mark was *not* going to show up. Miss Collins was going to think her debut show a failure. Thu and Dawson's Creek would never speak to each other—or *me*—again. Dad wasn't going to make it. And if Mom discovered what I'd done and then realized that Dad had blown it, she'd be upset too.

Sid and Emily were the only ones on my list that still had a chance. If Sid somehow made it back to his house within the next half hour, then at least one thing could go right tonight. But first, I had some rapid un-decorating to do.

I zipped downstairs to the dining room and promptly began tearing down all the romance. The special plates, the nicer silverware, the candles, the flowers... all of it. (On a side note, is there anything sadder than stuffing a fresh bouquet of roses into a trashcan?)

The pizza could stay. I just planned on leaving a note saying I decided to have a little adventure in cooking. Therefore, I ate a slice to make it look like it was for me. It tasted... okay? I mean, it was a 100% organic gluten free pizza loaded with vegetables. Not exactly Dominoes.

Finally, I took away the digital movie projector and returned it to my dad's study. This was the hardest part. I'd worked countless hours on this stupid movie. And now what? No one was ever going to see it? I stuffed the flash drive into my desk drawer.

Then: A text from Emily. My heart stopped.

EMILY: *Where ARE you guys?*

I waited a desperate minute before replying. After all, there was always a one percent chance Sid might show up at the last second...

ME: *Are you at Sid's house?*

EMILY: *Uh, yeah?? I'm supposed to be, right?*

Crap. She sounded pissed.

ME: *I'm so, so sorry. Something's kind of come up. I'm not sure when Sid will get there.*

Emily must have been a very talented texter, as her response came practically right on top of mine.

EMILY: *What does THAT mean? Are you guys coming or not?*

EMILY: *I skipped my friend's party for this.*

EMILY: *And why are Sid's parents screaming about math????*

ME: *I'm really sorry. Seriously. Wait a few more minutes? Please? I swear there's an explanation...*

EMILY: *I will wait ONE more minute.*

ME: *Thanks!*

Completely drained, I dragged myself back up to my room. *Mission Control.* What a joke. How could this have possibly happened? It wasn't fair. As for Sid and Emily, my grand scheme for them was supposed to have gone like this:

1.) Sid and I hang out in his room, recapping how amazingly successful everything had gone with The Plan.

2.) Emily shows up at his house "unexpectedly," for an impromptu rehearsal of *Zombie Apocalypse.*

3.) I receive an emergency text from Tad and excuse myself, leaving Sid and Emily to rehearse alone.

4.) I accidentally leave a copy of my script near Emily. It contains a partially edited love note from Sid to Emily. (I wrote it.)

5.) Emily is overwhelmed by the extremely well written prose and throws herself at Sid.

6.) Sid has no idea what's going on, but completely goes along with it because he's a boy.

7.) I return home to find my parents happy, and all is right with the world.

That's how things were *supposed* to go. Instead, they went like this:

EMILY: *You guys suck. I'm leaving.*

And that was it. The Plan was officially over. I'd never thought failure was even a possibility. Not like this.

Exhausted, I lumbered over to my bed and collapsed. My heart wasn't even in my stomach anymore. It was just gone. My eyes closed. I thought about crying, but couldn't. All I felt was empty. There was just a big nothing where all my working parts should've been.

I heard the garage door opening. Mom's grumbling muscle car was pulling into the driveway.

Great, I thought. *Now I have to pretend like everything's fine.*

I dragged myself off the bed and prepared to plaster a smile on my face. She was going to want to know how my day was. And also why I wasn't at Sid's. *Better think of a lie...*

I'd never felt so stupid. Hadn't I already discovered the truth about plans? They don't work. Never have. Never will.

Why couldn't I just take my own advice and be done with it?

SEVENTY-ONE DAYS

I WAS NEVER, ever leaving my room ever again. To heck with food. To heck with drink. I needed neither. All I required was a pillow. And Heinrich Von CuddleBear. My parents made frequent stops outside my door, knocking and asking if I was all right, to which I would reply with a heavy groan and a plea for solitude. Surprisingly, neither of them violated the "DO NOT ENTER" sign and settled for just talking to me through the door.

When they weren't pestering me, I passed the hours staring out the window. It was a crisp, sunny day outside, but somehow it seemed much darker. It was like there were tiny little shadows everywhere, and now that I'd noticed them, I couldn't un-notice them. It's strange how that works, isn't it? The world always reflects how you feel. If you're bright and happy, then it's bright and happy too. If you're sullen and miserable, then sullen and miserable is what you get back. Perhaps that's why the view of my backyard was looking so pitiful. It didn't matter how many birds chirped or how brightly the Sun shone, it all seemed downtrodden and grey.

Then, around noon, Sid started texting. I watched with gloomy disinterest as the little talk bubbles accumulated on the screen.

SID: Hey, where'd you go last night? I called you a million times.

SID: So…

SID: Yeah, that didn't work out with Thu and Pacey. Sorry about that.

SID: Thu almost killed me. She chased me with a fork!

SID: Can you believe that? An edged weapon!

SID: I don't think she was mad at *me*, per se. But that woman has a fury…

SID: Are you OK, by the way?

SID: I heard from Tad about your doctor not showing. That really sucks.

SID: He said the play was good though…

SID: If that helps?

SID: And Miss Collins invited them for tea afterwards.

SID: How'd things go with your parents?

SID: Hello?

SID: I'm sure that one worked out at least.

SID: Oh, by the way.

SID: Side note:

SID: Do you know why Emily texted me last night to "eat a bag of dicks?"

SID: That seemed weird.

SID: And who uses that expression anymore??

SID: Chloe, seriously, are you there?

SID: Just answer and I'll leave you alone.

SID: I promise.

SID: Okay, this isn't cool.

SID: Hello???

SID: Jeez, I just had to call your beautiful mother. She says you're in your room.

SID: Not cool not answering, dude.

SID: Anyway. I'm sorry about last night.

I clicked off the phone, never responding. I didn't know why, but I couldn't force myself to type anything. I needed complete and utter seclusion. Sid was just trying to check up on me, but somehow that only made me upset. (Not very nice of me, I know, but emotions are weird things.)

It wasn't the failure of The Plan that had me so down. I mean, that was *part* of it, obviously, but it definitely wasn't the whole picture. The whole picture was that the reality of my situation was beginning to sink in. There was nothing to distract me anymore. Because as long as I was running around playing matchmaker, then the Everywhere Cancer couldn't touch me. Now I was left with nothing but the truth. My life, and all the big swirly days within it, was going to end. Like really *end*, end. Nothing I, or anyone else could do, would change that. And somehow the scariest part was that the world would simply spin on, heedless, without me. Cloudy days, sunny days, days that were somewhere in between—they were all for other people now. All my hopes for creating something bright and beautiful in my wake had just been dashed. It was like the ocean or something—all those waves. Each and every one is forgotten as quickly as it arrives, replaced by another and then another and another. I guess that's life though. You're here and then you're not. Your friends remember you a while, but eventually their memories drift away like everything else.

A few weeks ago, Mr. Bowen mentioned "entropy" in class. Well, in case you were wondering, this is what entropy means. Everything fades. And for some of us, this happens a lot sooner than we'd like.

Now, I adore science. I really do. But sometimes I sure wish physics of this sort would just leave me the heck alone.

SIXTY-NINE DAYS

A COUPLE DAYS LATER, I violated my "never, ever leaving my room" policy, and went to school. It wasn't *entirely* my decision to do this. My parents gave me an ultimatum: either go to school, or schedule an emergency visit with Dr. Mark. I suppose their reasoning was that if I felt *physically* well enough to get out of bed, then I had to do it. But if I felt weak or nauseous or whatever else, then I needed to go to the hospital. Since I felt reasonably normal—and because I was still a little cross with Dr. Mark for flaking on Miss Collins—I opted for school. But that didn't mean I was happy about it.

Mom dropped me off a few minutes early, and my first instinct was to head to Mr. Sato's where I knew I'd find Sid and Thu. But then I remembered I didn't want to see anyone so I just wandered the halls aimlessly until the bell rang.

Once it did, classes began. I sat through each one like a ghost, not really listening and definitely not talking. After all, what was the point? Why bother to learn about trigonometry or the American Revolution or what F. Scott Fitzgerald truly *meant* by that green light across the bay? I mean, seriously. Who cares? Absolutely none of that stuff matters in the end. Heck, even if I didn't have Everywhere Cancer, it *still* wouldn't matter. Nothing does.

By lunchtime, I was practically a zombie. And as you might guess, I wasn't hungry at all. I even avoided Brick Wall Place. I went to the open benches instead, sitting by myself. And that's literally *all* I did. I just sat and stared at my feet. My mind was as blank as a cotton ball. Weird, random thoughts flitted through it. *How tall is the Empire State Building? Do they still make Juicy Fruit gum? I think I need new shoes.* My current pair of pink Converse looked like they'd been to hell and back. Maybe they could last a few more weeks? After all, they wouldn't need to last much longer than that.

Minutes rolled by in a haze. I was so lost in my own little world that I didn't even notice Sid and Thu hovering over me. I could barely even hear them. I was underwater and their voices were all muffled. I'm pretty sure, "what are you doing?" was the question that kept getting asked.

Eventually, I looked up blankly.

"I said, why are you sitting by yourself?" Sid asked.

"I don't need new shoes," I said.

Sid and Thu shared a glance. "Uh... let's go to Mr. Sato's. It's getting cold out here." Sid put out his hand.

I took it like an automaton and followed him to the warm classroom. All throughout, my fellow nerds were chatting, playing chess, studying, snacking and arguing over embarrassing topics like the actual number of parsecs it took Han Solo to complete the Kessel Run.

"You should've texted me back, you know," Sid said as we found an open table. He and Thu sat opposite me, both staring intently.

"Sorry," I said with a hollow, cracked voice. I looked at Thu. "Are you mad at us? Sid said you tried to kill him."

She blushed. "I didn't try to *kill* him. I just... chased him a little."

"With a deadly weapon," Sid added. "But no. We've reconciled. And as for your weak attempt at 'sorry,' I'm afraid it's not accepted. I was literally pulling my hair out I was so worried about you. I didn't know if you were in the hospital or..." he suddenly stopped and I looked up at him.

"Dead?" I asked.

Okay, that was a little uncalled for, but in all fairness, I was in a ridiculously uncalled for type of mood.

He turned a deep shade of crimson, just like Thu. "Mad at me," he said. "I was going to say 'mad at me.'"

"Well, I'm not," I answered flatly.

"I can see that," he said. "Look, are you all right? You don't seem like you."

Once again, my eyes shot up at him. "Like *me?*" I asked sharply. "And what does that even mean? How *should* I be acting?"

Thu looked away, embarrassed, but Sid continued to hold my gaze. "Well, not *mean,* would be a start. I've never seen you this way."

"Sorry to disappoint," I said.

"Look, things didn't go as planned," he said. "But we gave it our best shot. And it was *fun,* right? Besides, everything will work out. Don't worry."

I went back to staring at my hands and muttered, "I wasn't doing it for *fun.*"

He paused, his face softening a little. "I know," he said. "But that doesn't mean it wasn't. I mean, think about it. I'll be telling the tale of Thu trying to break the Punjab Café's window for the rest of me life."

Thu suddenly elbowed him, but he continued.

"Dawson's Creek learned an invaluable lesson about the female temperament. Tad got to Second Base following his date with Jen, *and* he's going to take Drama next year because he liked Miss Collins so much. And speaking of Miss Collins, she's *hot.* She'll find a guy before you know it. As for your parents… I've spent enough time with them to know they'll work it out. Trust me. Those two are good. And of course if it *doesn't* work out, your mom can always give me a call."

"*Ew.*" I instinctively winced at the mental image. Then I felt an infinitesimal bubble of laughter that I managed to suppress. I was still mad—definitely—but a small smile couldn't hurt, could it?

"You're so gross," I said.

He smiled at me triumphantly. "Indeed I am. Very gross. And just now, you're starting to look a little more like yourself. Isn't that right, Thu?"

Thu nodded brightly, and—I might add—with a bit of *smugness.*

Ugh. I looked between the two of them and settled on Sid's beaming face. It was like he'd just checkmated me into cheering up and he knew it. *The cocky bastard. What did I ever do to deserve him? Something very good, apparently…*

"So," I said, hoping to change the subject. "Tad got to Second Base, huh?"

SIXTY-SEVEN DAYS

SID WAS RIGHT, you know. Everything *would* work out. Thu and Dawson's Creek would move on. Miss Collins and Dr. Mark would find their soul mates. My parents would be all right. I just wanted to play a staring role in bringing those things about. (Well, not the Thu and Dawson's Creek moving on part. I still had high hopes for their getting back together.)

Either way, there wasn't much I could do about it now. Now it was time to focus on *now*. The present. Today. The moment. And at this moment, I was in Physics sitting next to Adam Worley as Mr. Bowen explained our latest experiment. We'd be doing it in pairs, which meant Me + Adam Worley = Awkward. It involved a couple graduated cylinders, a tiny measuring beaker—about the size of a shot glass—and several cups of different fruit juices.

"It's not an *experiment* exactly," Mr. Bowen said as he finished handing out the supplies. "It's more like a demonstration. You'll love it."

Adam picked up one of the juices and gave me a dapper, somewhat James Bondish nod, like he was raising a martini glass. I'd like to say that I did *not* giggle like a 12-year-old in response, but that would be a lie.

"So the juices have different densities," Mr. Bowen went on. "White Grape is heaviest, then orange, then pomegranate. If you pour them in that order, then they shouldn't mix. You'll have three separate layers: Clear, orange and red. Next, I want you to pour all the remaining grape juice into the second cylinder. It should be exactly three beakers worth."

Adam and I got to work. It only took a few seconds. The first cylinder was actually kind of pretty, with three neat layers like a fancy cake. The second cylinder was just clear, with white grape juice up to the halfway point.

"Perfect." Mr. Bowen nodded when we were all done. "So does anyone care to guess why we're pouring juice into graduated cylinders?"

I raised my hand. "To learn about mass?"

He pointed to me, and then smiled sheepishly. "Actually no. But that's a good idea too. Let me write that down." He skipped over to his desk and quickly jotted something on a scratch pad. "Yes," he said, springing back to the middle of the room. "Mass will be a lesson for another day. But today I want to talk about *dimensions.* So..." He clapped his hands. "How many dimensions are there?"

A girl to my left raised her hand. "Three?"

Mr. Bowen nodded again. "That's right. Three. But which is which? Is there a 'first' dimension or a 'second' or a 'third'?"

No one answered.

"Take a look at your two cylinders," Mr. Bowen continued. "Both contain exactly three beakers of juice, right? For the mixed one, it's easy to tell them apart. You can point to beaker number one, beaker number two and beaker number three. But what about the grape juice cylinder? We know that there *are* three beakers in it, but it makes no sense to ask which one is which. The whole thing's just clear. There's no beaker number one, or beaker number two. Everyone with me?"

I looked around the room and saw a few nods.

"Well," Mr. Bowen said. "It's the same with dimensions. There are three of them, but we can't point to which one is which. Now, for the final bit of the demonstration, I want you to pour the remainder of your pomegranate juice into the white grape cylinder. See how it rests on top? *That*, ladies and gentlemen, is a *fourth* dimension. It's actually really simple. The three dimensions we're all familiar with, the Cartesian coordinates of length, width and breadth, are *spatial* dimensions. A fourth dimension, like 'time' for example, is a temporal one. It behaves in a different way, and that's why we can tell it apart from the first three. It's like that final layer of pomegranate. It's a dimension too, but a different density. Get it?"

I honestly wasn't sure if I completely got it or not, but I definitely laughed along with the rest of the class. Mr. Bowen, by the time he'd finished his explanation was practically dancing in circles. I mean, seriously. When he talked like this, his hair literally poofed up with an extra jolt of electricity. Plus, he was about a light year away from the textbook. Our current chapter was on "rotational motion," which was sort of interesting, I guess, but also sort of boring. Dimensions were far cooler.

"Anyway," Mr. Bowen concluded. "My hope is that some-day, if any of you become Physics majors, you'll stumble onto this little thing called 'String Theory.' It'll talk about how there are actually *nine* dimensions—or even more in some versions—and you'll understand just what the heck it's talking about. Now,"—he picked up one of the cylinders—"Bottoms up!"

Adam looked over at me with raised eyebrows. His expression sort of read: *Wow. This guy's crazy!*

"My lady," he said graciously. "You want the triple flavor or the double?"

It took me a second to realize he was referring to the drinks. "The triple," I said, and then we cheersed graduated cylinders.

After a moment, Adam looked at me, bemused. "Cartesian coordinates?" he said, gulping his last swallow. "We're in high school, right? I mean, it's almost like he's putting... *Descartes* before the horse?"

He then paused hopefully, waiting to see if I might get it.

And yes, after a moment of shock, I definitely got it. Seventeenth Century mathematician, René Descartes, was the guy who invented the Cartesian coordinate system, which is still in use today. It was the type of thing that only a very, very serious super nerd would know.

"Adam," I said hesitantly, not quite sure if I should look up at him or not. "That was, um..." I paused and then finally met his eyes. "I mean... that was the lamest joke I've ever heard!"

"Thank you." He beamed and put on a cool, Zeus-like pose. "I'm full of bad jokes," he added proudly. "I was terrified you wouldn't get it. Just don't ask me why koala bears aren't actual bears. Cause that's a tough one."

"Um..."

"Okay, fine. They don't have the koalafications."

I laughed. "That was worse!"

He smiled again, and I thought: *Yes, Adam Worley. Just in case you were wondering, the answer is yes. You are awesome and I'm totally in love with you.*

"Tell me one more!" I squealed.

126

SIXTY-SIX DAYS

THE NEXT DAY in Drama, I had to keep fighting to stay upright as we made it through our final round of rehearsals. Opening night for *Zombie Apocalypse: A Love Story* was tomorrow night. I had all my lines thoroughly memorized since… well, I didn't really *have* any lines. Or at least, any lines with actual words. My role was more of a footwork thing. Basically, I was the world's clumsiest member of the undead, tripping and falling a total of fourteen times throughout a one-hour play.

Sid and Emily, however, were having serious problems. Emily was still harboring a bit of murderous rage following The Plan debacle, and Sid was growing increasingly frustrated.

And poor Miss Collins. She was so full of jitters, zipping around the room to make sure everyone was getting everything right. I worried that her usual poise might have been shaken by the recent "failure" of her comedy show in the city. I wanted to tell her it was all my fault and confess what I'd done. Yet somehow the opportunity never came. There were always too many people around, and I knew if I startled babbling my apology it would come out wrong and make things worse.

Plus, I was a lot more nervous than I thought I'd be. My heart was absolutely pounding and I was sweating all over. For the past couple months, I kept comforting myself with the knowledge that I didn't have to actually *say* anything while on stage. Still, my stomach kept twisting in knots, and more than once, I felt like I was going to throw up. I did my best to hide it, but it was getting tougher.

"Chloe?" Miss Collins said, now zipping in my direction. "Are you all right?"

I swallowed. "Yes, Miss Collins."

She regarded me skeptically. "Dear, you look really pale. Would you like to come sit?"

"I'm okay, really," I lied. "I'm just nervous."

Miss Collins spun around to face the rest of the class. "Don't just stand there, you lot. Act two, scene four! Set it up!"

Everyone scurried to their marks while Miss Collins quietly pulled me aside. "Chloe," she said in a lowered voice. "I'd like you to see the nurse, okay?"

"But I'm fine," I said.

Her features softened a bit. "You're very brave, dear, I know that. But I'm afraid this isn't a request." She then turned and called for Sid in a loud voice. "Would you come here a moment, please?"

He ran over, looking relieved to be away from Emily's stony glare. He arrived, panting a little. "What's up?" he asked.

"I'm sending Chloe to Nurse Jacobs," Miss Collins told him. "I'd like you to go with her."

"Miss Collins!" I protested again.

"Dear, it will only take a moment. Besides, you've nailed your role better than anyone I think. The last thing you need is more rehearsals." She turned to Sid. "You know where the nurse's office is?"

He nodded.

"Good. Wait with her until Miss Jacobs dismisses you. Understand?"

Sid nodded again and looked at me with a shrug. "Never pass up on a chance to skip class, I always say."

"You've never said that," I said with a glare.

"Sure I have. Anyway, let's go."

"You know I'm really okay," I said to both of them, even though—as much as I hated to admit it—the nausea was getting worse.

"Just have her take a look at you," Miss Collins repeated. "Now run along. Tell her I sent you."

With that, Sid took my arm and gently guided me toward the door. I followed, keeping my eyes pinned to my feet. It was like they were stuck there by an invisible string. I'd never felt so embarrassed and ashamed. It didn't make any sense to feel that way, but that's how I felt. And as we left, I could literally feel everyone staring at us.

"You look good to me," Sid offered once we were out in the hall.

"Why'd she have to *do* that?" I asked bitterly.

"Teachers," Sid said with another shrug. "Can't trust a one of them."

Before long, we'd made it to Nurse Jacobs' office. She was an older lady with short, curly white hair and half-moon glasses. She shuffled around the room and asked what she could do for us.

Before I could answer, Sid told her, "Miss Collins wanted you to take a look at Chloe."

"Which is totally unnecessary," I muttered.

"Well, let's have you get up here," Nurse Jacobs said, patting the exam table.

Stiffly, I hobbled over and hopped up. Nurse Jacobs began getting out the usual "doctor's office" stuff, i.e. blood pressure thingy, thermometer, stethoscope, etc...

She was in the middle of frowning at the results on the thermometer when I felt a horrible twist in my chest and a rush of heat swept my face. The all-too-familiar sense of imminent puking hit me like a ton of bricks.

"*Sorry!*" I immediately squeaked, and shot off the table toward the nearest waste bucket.

• • •

Dr. Mark swept into the exam room with his usual flare, eyeing my lab results as he walked. Mom was standing beside me, gripping my hand a little too tightly for comfort. (The woman seriously needed to stop working out so much…)

"My favorite foot soldier," Dr. Mark said, setting my chart aside. He took a seat on his stool, making the thing look comically small, and scooted over to my side. "How are you feeling?" he asked.

"Better now," I said.

"That's good. Also, before I forget, I wanted to tell you I couldn't make it to that play last week. I'm really sorry but there was an emergency at the hospital." He looked at me with a plea for forgiveness. "If it's any consolation," he added. "I'm pretty sure I saved a young boy's life?"

He didn't know that I'd had spies outside the theater that night, so of course I already knew he missed it. I gave him a weak smile, and said, "I guess I can forgive you in that case."

"Please," Mom said. "Just tell us how she's doing. I mean, she looks a lot better, right? Her color's back and everything. Was this just a hiccup?"

Dr. Mark nodded again and took a deep breath. He glanced at my mom and then at me. "Your labs are pretty much what I'd expect at this point," he said. "I'll be honest, they're not *great*. But they're not horrible either."

"What does that *mean?!*" Mom suddenly barked, startling me. Her tone had taken on a significantly sharper edge than I was used to. She hardly ever got angry like that, and definitely not with Dr. Mark.

"Look," he said, keeping his eyes level. "I'm truly sorry. I really am. If you'd like, we can go over each test specifically, and I can explain what they all mean. The summary, though, is that a lot of the different ranges are below where I'd like to see them. And basically what that means is that, Chloe, you're going to have to take it easy. More rest. Less physical exertion.

And it's up to you, but I'd recommend staying home from school."

My face fell in shock. Stay home from school? Like, *permanently?* No. I couldn't do that. Staying home meant the *end*. It meant that "normal" was all over. I mean, I felt *better*. I really did. There wasn't any difference between the me of today and the me of yesterday. So why change anything now?

Dr. Mark seemed to read my mind and quickly added, "Again, that's just my recommendation. You don't *have* to stay home. If you do, however, that will likely give you more..." he stopped short, tossing a guilty look toward my mom.

"What?" she asked.

"...time," he said.

The hand gripping mine suddenly tightened so hard I thought my fingers might break.

SIXTY-FIVE DAYS

"BUT I *WANT* TO DO IT!" I screeched, balling my fists. "Why is that so hard to understand?"

Mom's face remained frozen in sympathy, yet unrelenting. "Honey, please," she said evenly. "Don't make this any harder than it has to be, okay?"

"*I'm* the one making it difficult?" I screamed back.

"Sweetheart," Dad said. "We've already spoken to the principal and your Drama teacher. If a student is absent from class, then they aren't allowed to participate in the performance. Those are the rules."

"But *you're* the one who made me stay home! I told you I felt fine!"

My parents exchanged a glance. My dad hesitated, as if awaiting telepathic confirmation that he and Mom were on the same page. "We could go *watch* the play if you want?" he said.

Admittedly, this was a semi-reasonable proposal but I was in no mood to compromise.

"We don't have tickets!" I said, stomping. "And do you know why? Because I'm supposed to be *in* it!"

"I'm sure they'll let us in..."

"No! Just forget it. This is so completely stupid anyway. Thank you both very, very much!"

With that, I stormed out of the kitchen and flew up the stairs to my room. Slamming the door, I threw myself onto the bed and sobbed into my pillow. I couldn't believe this was happening. I'd been rehearsing for months, and even though I was nervous, it was a good kind of nervous. I *wanted* to do it. I wanted to be part of it. I was Zombie Number One! Plus, I felt *fine*. I didn't have any nausea, or dizziness, or lightheadedness or whatever other stupid thing. But because my stupid parents were so freaked out by stupid Dr. Mark, they made me stay home from school. Now I was going to miss *everything!* The whole stupid play and everyone in it. Can't anything just go the way it's supposed to? For *once???*

I mean, I was a good person, right? I didn't do anything wrong. I was a normal kid! I was nice! And then one day in sixth grade I didn't feel well and BAM! EVERYWHERE CANCER!

Now here I am. Five years later and nobody can do a stupid thing.

And what in the world will staying home accomplish?

"*More time,*" Dr. Mark had said. More time for what? Sitting around doing nothing? Lying in bed all day? Feeling like crap?

Time, indeed.

I hated *everyone*. None of them could ever understand this. How could they? They still had *decades* in front of them. I had *weeks*.

They were all idiots. Stupid parents. Stupid doctors. Stupid teachers. Stupid *Sid*. Walking me to the nurse's office like that, not even standing up for me at all! What was he thinking? If he cared about me even the slightest bit he would've refused—he would have told her I was fine. Which I was! GOD DAMN IT!

I felt a sudden heat and ran to the bathroom to throw up.

SIXTY-FOUR DAYS

I WOKE UP the next morning to a pile of messages from Sid. Apparently he'd been texting continuously since the end of the play last night. Blearily, I read through them.

SID: Zombie Apocalypse finito!

SID: I can't believe it's over

SID: It was actually a bust

SID: Jessica Alvarez filled in for you and SUCKED

SID: By my count, she ruined 68.5% of the jokes. Never in the right place at the right time. We needed Chloe Cartwright.

SID: But on a happier note…

SID: Emily Sulecki's in love with me again.

SID: She gave a very convincing performance

SID: Too convincing

SID: She wants me badly

SID: Smoldering eyes

SID: Flushed bosom

SID: Her soul burns with the passion of a thousand suns and needs to be quenched with a little Siddhartha

SID: Anyway.

SID: It's like two in the morning now

SID: I hope ur doing ok

SID: Text me when you get up

SID: Nighty night

SID: Don't let the bedbugs bite.

SID: Wow, that's actually really gross. Why do people say that, anyway?

SID: I mean, *bedbugs?* Christ.

SID: Yeah, sweet dreams now, huh?

SID: If I could take back these last few texts, I would.

SID: The phone company needs to get on that.

SID: Sorry.

SID: Sleep tight?

Fighting to suppress a smile, I decided to type back. I was still in a foul mood, but figured a response wouldn't kill me.

ME: You still there?

It was only 7:02am on a Saturday, so I had to ask. I hadn't even needed to set the *Falcon* either. I just woke up automatically. My mother had done her work well. Anyway, Sid's response was practically immediate.

SID: Yep.

SID: How you feeling?

ME: Okay.

(Lie.)

SID: I guess you saw about Jessica Alvarez then?

ME: Yeah. I doubt she sucked. But thanks anyway.

SID: She did suck. I'm not just saying that either. The reviews were unanimous.

SID: Truly terrible.

SID: And I've never liked her.

ME: Didn't you ask her to be your girlfriend last year?

SID: She's a horrible person.

ME: Right.
ME: Anyway. How did the play go? Like, seriously?

SID: Okay. Not too many people showed up. I guess they had better things to do.

ME: Was Miss Collins upset?

SID: No, she was cool.
SID: Actually she was great. I've never seen a woman more relieved. Or possibly stoned.

ME: I still feel bad about her play in SF. I need to tell her what happened.

SID: I told her.

ME: You WHAT?
ME: You told her???

SID: Relax.
SID: No names were given.
SID: I just told her the tickets were all purchased in an elaborate scheme to fix her up on a date.
SID: She looked semi-pissed for a second, but then laughed and called me a "cheeky bugger."
SID: It's all good.

ME: A cheeky bugger?

SID: Yeah.
SID: It's a term of endearment. I googled it.

ME: I'm honestly not sure what to say…

SID: Trust me.
SID: She's cool. I swear.

ME: Okay…
ME: Thanks.
ME: I guess.
ME: She really wasn't pissed??

SID: Of course not. She's British.

ME: ?

SID: Keep calm and carry on and all that.
SID: Just give her some tea and she'll be fine.
SID: That's the way it's done over there.

ME: And you'd know this because…?

SID: I'm Indian. But I hold no grudges.

ME: Um…
ME: Oh wait. I get it.

SID: Yeah. So what are you doing today?

ME: Lying in bed.
ME: Doctor's orders.

SID: That sucks.
SID: Wishing Adam Worley was there?

ME: Who?

SID: Who?

ME: You mean the lacrosse player guy?

SID: Seriously?

SID: That's how you're gonna play it?

SID: You practically admitted to being in love with him already.

SID: Remember that?

SID: After the concert?

ME: No I didn't.

SID: Yes you did.

ME: No I didn't.

SID: Yes you did.

(Very lengthy pause as I consider my options...)

ME: Okay fine.

ME: I kind of like him I guess.

ME: Maybe.

ME: But not a lot or anything.

ME: Just a smidge.

ME: Like if I were drawing a chart on how much I liked him, the line would only be a molecule high.

ME: Maybe two. I don't know.

SID: I'm sure he'd be flattered to hear that.

ME: Whatever.

ME: Tell me about Emily.

ME: She likes you now?

SID: Ah! Nice sudden and unprovoked topic change!

SID: And yes. She's in love with me. She can no longer conceal her true feelings.

ME: See? I told you she likes you. What did she do?

SID: She slapped me.

ME: Um…

SID: Big time. She's stronger than she looks too.

ME: Are you being serious?

SID: Oh yeah.
SID: It was during a costume change.
SID: You know the one near the end? Where me and her become zombies?

ME: Yeah.

SID: So when she was changing her shirt I went up to her and told her "thanks for not screwing up the lines."

ME: Very gallant.
ME: And pervy, btw.

SID: I meant it as a joke.
SID: Sort of.
SID: Anyway.
SID: She growled at me.
SID: Like a jungle cat.
SID: A tigress.

ME: Did you just write "tigress?"

SID: It's the most apt description.
SID: But don't get me sidetracked.
SID: So then I noticed this piece of debris in her hair.
SID: And I just wanted to help, so I brushed it out and she slapped me.
SID: Awesome, right?

ME: Um. Yeah?

SID: No yeah-question mark. This is yeah-exclamation point.

SID: I'll explain it for you.

SID: She slapped me, right? Like it was an instinct. She probably didn't even think about it. It just happened.

ME: So?

SID: So it's obvious.

SID: She has so much pent up desire that she's all wound up like a spring.

SID: She can barely contain herself. I was lucky she didn't start tearing my clothes off.

SID: Trust me. I know these things.

ME: And if she knees you in the balls next time?

SID: First of all, I'd block it.

SID: Second of all, I'd view such an action as a clear sign that she wants to do the nasty.

ME: Oh my god.

ME: Please don't say "do the nasty" ever again.

ME: So gross...

SID: Not to Emily I'm not. I'm like a giant cupcake on her birthday.

SID: With sprinkles.

SID: And she wants a piece.

SID: A big piece.

ME: Aaaaand I'm gonna barf.

SID: Beauty's in the eye of the beholder, young Chloe.

SID: Just watch and learn.

SID: At some point, she'll take a bite. You'll see.

ME: Ugh. Well. Best of luck with that. I hope she does.

ME: Take a bite.

ME: Or whatever.

SID: Hope has nothing to do with it.

SID: Hey, do you realize we've been texting for almost an hour?

ME: Wow. You're right.

SID: You know I could've just pressed "call" and the whole thing would've been done in like two minutes?

ME: Ha.

ME: Yeah.

ME: Well.

ME: We live in futuristic times.

SID: True.

ME: I think I have to go eat breakfast now anyway.

ME: It smells like eggs.

ME: And thanks, btw.

SID: For?

ME: Texting me.

SIXTY-TWO DAYS

OKAY, SO NOW I DEFINITELY FELT like a pile of crud. It was like I had the flu on steroids—tired, dizzy, aching all over, and wishing it were the distant future already so I could just go to the store and buy a new body.

Like *Battlestar Galactica*. Ever seen that show? Whenever the evil Cylons have a problem they can just "die" and immediately download into a fresh body. I mean, jeez. Wouldn't that be the life? *Got a headache?* New body. *Scrape your knee?* Heck with the band-aid. Gimme a new body!

Although for the record, I'd still like to be a person, and not like, you know, a killer robot. (Which is what the Cylons are.)

Anyway. Today was Monday and also my first official Not Going To School Anymore day. As you might imagine, I was pretty peeved about it. I mean, I know most teenagers would be thrilled to ditch class indefinitely. In fact, a magical "Ditch School Forever Pass" almost sounds like the premise to a bad Disney movie. It all depends on the circumstances though. There's a big, big difference between choosing not to do something, and not being *able* to do it.

What I *was* able to do, however, was preempt the incoming Wookie Roar from my bedside table as the *Millennium Falcon* hovered on the edge of 6:59. I stared at the numbers a moment, blinking. Then, with great effort, I levered my head from the pillow with a crowbar and swung my feet to the floor. *God, my entire body was made out of lead. Or actually, what's heavier than lead? Iridium? Yes. I was made out of iridium.*

As I rubbed my eyes, I could already hear the sounds of my parents and baby brother in the kitchen. It sounded like the usual frenzied breakfast routine, while the smell of fresh quinoa wafted up to my nose. (Tasty, right?)

I shuffled toward the bathroom with a heavy groan and then went downstairs to greet the day. Everyone was exactly as I figured they'd be. Mom was juggling food prep and Henry, shuttling between the stove and his high chair in a constant loop. Dad was highly distracted by something on his computer while he attempted to eat a granola bar. (I say "attempted" because he kept missing his mouth.) Henry's face was smeared with blackberry jam.

"Morning," I announced as I walked in.

Dad looked up, startled. "Oh, hey," he said quickly. "I was about to come get you."

"Morning sweetie," Mom called over her shoulder.

I took a seat and looked across the table to find Henry challenging me to a staring contest. (Normally, I would've crushed him, but today my head hurt so much I quickly conceded defeat.)

Then, out of nowhere, I announced, "I've always loved quinoa." I didn't necessarily *intend* to sound sarcastic, but it came out that way anyway.

Mom frowned as she completed another loop. "It has lots of antioxidants," she said. "Try to eat some. It'll help you feel better."

Dad stayed focused on his laptop, but distractedly noted, "I'm going to google 'antioxidant' once and for all. I've never understood…" His voice trailed off.

"So I'm taking Henry to daycare in a minute," Mom said as she forked some fruit onto her plate. "But after that, I'm taking a much needed break from the gym. I was thinking we might hang out today? Just the two of us?"

I couldn't help but scrunch my nose a little. For some reason the thought of "just the two of us" struck me as a little uncomfortable. What did "hang out" even imply? Did she want to do some sort of aerobic thing? I got a sudden mental image of yoga mats in the living room and weird, unpleasant stretching exercises. Plus, I was supposed to be resting. Wasn't that why I was staying home in the first place?

"Um, okay," I said hesitantly. "What did you have in mind?"

She forked a bite of cantaloupe and considered this a moment. "I don't know," she said lightly. She chewed for a second and then added, "Do you know I've never seen *Star Wars?* Like *any* of them?"

Yes. Yes, I did know that. One of the unfortunate aspects of my relationship with my mother was that we basically had *nothing* in common. She liked rock climbing; I liked videogames. She liked fitness; I liked spaceships. She liked CNN; I liked Dungeons & Dragons. I mean, it wasn't a huge deal or anything. We still got along okay. But if I were being completely honest, it did kind of bug me sometimes.

"I have the whole series plus Bonus Features on Blu-ray," I offered. "You're welcome to borrow it any time. I've told you that for years."

She frowned. "That's true, but,"—she paused, thinking—"I think I need a guide. A Jedi Master. So to speak."

Oh?

Oh.

"You mean...?"

She smiled. "I'm thinking it's marathon time. What do you say?"

I was actually thrilled, but managed to keep an excellent poker face. "Depends," I said. "Do I get authority over the snack menu?"

From the sudden wrinkle in her nose, I could tell she hadn't considered this. Then, as if conceding defeat, she said, "Tell you what. We play Paper, Rock, Scissors for every snack choice. If you win, you pick. If I win, I pick. Deal?"

I said, "deal," and we shook on it.

A second later, totally randomly, Dad started reading aloud from his laptop. "An antioxidant is a molecule that inhibits the oxidation of other molecules. Oxidation is a chemical reaction that can produce free radicals, which may damage cells." He looked up. "That *does* sound healthy."

Mom and I exchanged a glance. "So…" I said. "I'll get the movies?"

"Sounds like a plan."

Roughly two hours later, we were curled up on the couch with numerous fluffy blankets and well into *A New Hope*. Multiple rounds of Paper, Rock, Scissors had yielded an impressive spread of buttered popcorn, a jumbo-sized bag of Cheetos, two half-eaten cartons of chocolate ice cream, and yes, a single bag of Kale chips. (I hadn't lost; I'd simply been magnanimous in victory.)

Also, Mom hadn't been kidding when she said she needed a guide. She had *endless* questions.

"But if the prequels come first, why don't we start there?"

"Because they suck. But they're still *Star Wars*. So they're good."

"Why are the bad guys wearing those awkward suits?"

"They're Stormtroopers. That's their uniform."

"Like body armor?"

"Apparently not."

"Why didn't Obi-Wan approach Luke sooner?"

"He was waiting for the Force."

"What's the Force?"

"A mystical energy that binds the universe. Pay no attention to the explanation in the prequels."

"Is the annoying robot going to be in all three movies?"

"C-3PO. And yes. Unfortunately."

"Hey, that's your alarm clock!"

"The *Millennium Falcon*."

"What's the Kessel Run?"

"A smuggling route."

"Why do they use light swords?"

"Light*sabers*. They're more civilized."

"Chopping people's arms off?"

"Yes."

"Can I have some of those Cheetos?"

"Seriously?"

"There's no way he could block those laser blasts! It looks like he's playing tennis!"

"Yes he can! He's a Jedi!"

"Sweetie, he'd have to move faster than light. That's impossible."

"He's using the Force!"

"I still don't get what the Force is."

"*Ugh!*"

"I like Han Solo."

"Me too."

"He's kinda hot."

"I agree."

• • •

By the afternoon, we'd nearly made it through the entire original trilogy. Oddly enough, it was me who fell asleep first. I passed out somewhere during the Death Star battle in *Return of the Jedi*. (In my defense, I'd already seen it like a hundred times.) When I woke up it was dark outside. I'd been moved to my bed at some point and was positively covered in blankets. The *Falcon* read 8:53. I grinned and rolled over.

Not a bad day, I thought warmly, and then promptly fell back asleep.

FIFTY-NINE DAYS

THREE DAYS LATER it was my birthday. (Notice the significant lack of fanfare to this announcement.) Basically, the nice way to describe my party was that it was "low key." By that, I mean there wasn't a party. I felt way too sick to do anything fun, let alone be sociable. Sid, Thu and Tad came over for a bit (no Dawson's Creek), but that was about it. I did my best to appear upbeat, but it was tough—a lot tougher than I thought it would be. So... not much of a party. Everyone left after an hour. They all made excuses like they'd only planned to stay for a few minutes because they had a "thing" to get to or studying to get done, but it was pretty obvious.

I felt guilty after they left, like I'd just made everyone totally uncomfortable. I mean, it wasn't my fault, but still... I felt stupid.

Anyway. I was now sixteen years of age. Yipee.

• • •

And so the weeks passed. The weather got colder—like actual *winter* cold—and most days I felt like a living pile of mud. The sickness just went on and on. High temperature, nausea, dizziness, aching, the whole works. It never ended. And let me tell you, there is something uniquely awful about feeling bad and never improving. Like, usually when you get sick, you feel crappy for a few days and then get better. But when you feel terrible for weeks on end with no breaks, it literally saps the life out of you. People kept telling me to "stay positive," but positivity needs *fuel*. It's like a fire. It needs more coal or logs or whatever else to keep it going. If it doesn't get them, it burns out. No way around it.

After a while, my days at home developed into a routine. I started sleeping past seven for once, usually getting up around ten. I'd choke down a smoothie and then take a nap, then watch TV, then try to eat, then read, then work on Henry's letter. (The one part of The Plan where I could still salvage something.) Unfortunately, I couldn't write at Hiding Hill anymore. The short bike ride was too far to pedal now. I could barely make it up and down the stairs. So instead, I just worked on it in my room. Mom kept asking what I was writing, but for some reason, I'd decided to keep it a secret. I'd tell her, "just a diary," and that seemed to satisfy her.

And speaking of Hiding Hill, I hadn't seen Hank in *forever*. It had been weeks. I mean, even if I wasn't going over to his favorite spot anymore, I at least expected to see him lurking outside my window or something. But he was nowhere to be found. Kind of like everyone else for that matter. After my birthday, hardly anyone ever called or visited. Sid and Thu would text occasionally, but that was it. And they were sparse texts too, just saying things like "how r u?" and then nothing more. It was weird. I mean, I'm sure they had their reasons and everything. Final exams were coming up, and everyone was busy applying to colleges, so they were probably super busy. Still, I couldn't help but feel left behind. They were all moving forward with their lives and I was standing still. Or actually, I was *lying* still, spending half my days cooped up in my room and lying in bed.

Most days I wondered: *Are they practicing for when I'm gone? Are they getting used to it?*

I didn't blame them if that's what they were doing. I really didn't. They had their own lives to worry about—their own futures. I didn't want to drag anyone down. Plus, it was probably super awkward to see me in my current state. Most days I could barely get out of bed, let alone be good company. I just lay there like a sloth. Besides, what could they do? Just sit in my room for hours? So, yeah. I guess it was only natural that they stayed away. I'd probably do the same. It was just human nature.

To be honest, though, that didn't stop it from breaking my heart. At least, a little.

THIRTY-FIVE DAYS

OKAY, SO I'M NOT SURE how to say this without exploding into a million glittery sparkles, but… okay here it is: After years and years of thinking that this was a complete and utter impossibility, and that it would need to stay confined to the realm of my imagination—ADAM WORLEY ASKED ME OUT.

That's right. You didn't read that wrong. Adam "Koala Jokes" Worley asked me on a date. Can you believe it? I mean, the epicness of this epic event was so epic I could barely even remember it happening. All I knew was the result, which was that I was now standing nervously outside my house wearing a *dress*—something that's only happened once in history—and waiting for him to pick me up. I kept shuffling my feet and hopping from one to the other so much, it was like I was dancing. I couldn't believe this day had finally arrived. He hadn't told me where we were going either. It was a surprise.

Then, appearing from a curl of mist, his truck came gliding down the street. He pulled up to the curb and stepped out, trotting around to open my door and help me up. (The truck was kinda tall.)

And I'll just say this: *Jesus Almighty he was handsome!* He was wearing blue jeans and a red flannel button up, which on some guys might look hipster, but on him was distinctly cowboyish.

"Hey there, beautiful," he said, taking my hand.

I tucked a stray lock behind my ear, totally not missing the fact that he'd just call me beautiful. "Hi," I said.

He smiled and helped me into the cab. "Watch your step," he added.

With a jaunty bounce to his stride, he ran back around to the driver's side and got in.

"So," he said. "Wondering where we're going?"

Resuming my intense examination of my hands, I answered, "Um, kinda?"

"Well don't you worry, darlin'," he said, doing his best country accent. "I'm old school. There's this great little Italian restaurant downtown."

"I like Italian," I said, perking up.

"I know."

And with that, we were off. I couldn't help stealing glances at him every few seconds. I mean, he was just so perfect. His face, those dimples, his shoulders, that spicy shampoo… The whole thing felt surreal. How did this even *happen*, anyway? It was like I was the luckiest girl in the whole world and couldn't remember how.

"I really like that dress by the way," he said, taking his eyes from the road a moment. "How come you never wear it to school?"

"I kind of… *can't.*"

"You can't?"

I swallowed. This was where I was about to totally embarrass myself. "Um. Her name's Martha, actually," I said. "She's my reserve dress."

He looked at me again with tiny crinkles around his eyes. "Reserve dress?"

"Yes," I said with a new firmness and jut my chin a little. "Every girl needs a reserve dress. I keep her in her own special closet. Like the Batsuit for Batman."

"I see," he said, frowning for a moment before giving me an oddly sheepish look. "This is kind of embarrassing to admit, but see this shirt I'm wearing? It's *my* reserve shirt. His name's Jim."

I smile crept across my face. He was definitely making fun of me now. "Shut up," I said in a small voice.

"No, I'm serious," he insisted. "Have you ever seen me wear it before?"

"No."

"See? I'm telling you. Jim only makes it out for special occasions."

I looked at him. "Really?"

He raised an eyebrow and the laughter crinkles returned.

Yep. Definitely messing with me. "Okay fine," I said. "You're a boy, I get it."

He chuckled and then shrugged. "It's actually not a bad idea though. Reserve Shirt. I like that."

Grinning, I turned away and rolled down my window. It was almost dark, but the night was still warm and summerlike. I briefly closed my eyes and let the wind brush my face. Opening them, I couldn't help but notice how empty the neighborhood was. At first I just thought it was a slow night, but the more I looked, the more I realized no one was on the road. There weren't any other cars at all. No bikes. No pedestrians. No one. It was just me and Adam.

I briefly considered mentioning this, but decided against it. I just wanted to enjoy the night.

"This is it," he announced as we pulled in front of the restaurant. He shut off the engine and hopped out, running around to get my door. I smiled at the sight of him looking so cute.

"Thanks," I said, letting him take my hand again as he helped me down. "I think I've seen this place before."

"It's supposed to be really good," he said. I then noticed with a pounding heart that even though I was out of the truck, he had yet to let go of my hand. "Shall we?" He gestured.

"Yes."

We walked together inside. It was dim with flickering candles and soft music, and also, like the streets, completely empty.

"Well, this is weird," Adam said after a pause.

"Should we go somewhere else?" I asked.

"But the reviews…" he said quietly, then straightened. "Let's check the kitchen."

He let go of my hand and trotted toward the back where he disappeared through a pair of double doors. A moment later he reappeared, looking shocked. "Chloe, check this out."

"What?" I asked, skipping over.

"The kitchen's empty, but there's all this food prepared. Look."

My eyes widened when I saw it. There were at least a dozen fresh plates of steaming pasta with wine, bread, cheese, olives…

"I don't get it," I said, scrunching my nose. "Was this all made, like, recently?"

"Looks like it." He turned to face me with eyes that glinted with a familiar mischief. "So…" he said slowly. "Shall we?"

I laughed. "You mean you still want to eat here?"

"Why not?" He whirled around and swept up a plate of linguini. "For you, miss," he said. "Unless of course you'd prefer the…" He scanned the rest of the entrees. "Oysters?" he asked.

I squirmed involuntarily. "Ugh, now way," I said. "I'll stick with the non-slimy pasta, thanks."

"As you wish." He bowed and handed over the plate.

Once we were seated—a cozy table for two with a tiny candle glowing between us—I said, "So, can I ask you a question?"

"Of course," he answered.

"How come you asked me out?"

He suddenly scowled in that way that boys do when they're confused. "What do you mean?"

"I don't know," I said. "I just mean... you're like, *Adam Worley*. You could ask out anyone. Why me?"

He rubbed his chin a moment as he considered this. Then, after an interminable pause, he asked, "You really want the truth?"

"Um, yeah?" I said.

"Well... the truth is I lost a bet. Going out with you was the penalty."

He said it with such deadpan seriousness that I just sat there blinking for an eternity until he boomed, "Okay, that sounded way funnier in my head!" He held up his hands in surrender. "I swear that was supposed to sound like banter."

Still stunned, my hand inadvertently grabbed an olive and threw it at him.

"I'm sorry!" He laughed again. "I was kidding, I swear. But do you still want the truth?"

I narrowed my eyes. "I'm not so sure anymore."

"I *like* you, Chloe," he said. "I mean, I could go through a whole list of reasons if you want. Like how you make me laugh, or how you get my bad jokes—minus the last one of course— but the truth is actually pretty simple. Whenever you're not around, I wish you were. I actually *look forward* to going to Physics, can you believe that? And I can't help it either. I think even if I were mad at you, I'd *still* want you around." He then blushed a little, and looked at me with a pained face. "Does that make me sound weird? It does, doesn't it?"

Before I could answer with a sudden and resounding, "*No, that does not make you weird at all and I love you too!*" there was a loud clatter from the kitchen. It sounded like a jumble of pots crashing to the floor. We both jumped and Adam stood up. "Wait here," he said quietly, slowly creeping toward the double doors. As he walked, there was another loud *clang,* and then another and another.

"Adam, let's just…" I started to say, but he half-turned and put a finger to his lips.

I started to get up as I watched him inch forward. When he got to the doors, he slowly pushed them open and ducked inside. I stood as still as a statue, listening. The clangs and crashes had stopped. The restaurant was dead quiet except for the soft music playing overhead. I stepped backward, instinctively moving toward the exit.

Then, with a thunderous shout, Adam exploded through the doors. His face was ashen as he bolted toward me and screamed, "RUN!"

Paralyzed, I stayed still until he grabbed my wrist and yanked me along.

"Adam, what—?" I tried to scream, but he cut me off.

"Just run!"

So I ran. I'd never run so hard in my life, especially since I was keeping up with a boy twice my size. The dark streets were a blur as we passed window after window, breathing hard under the sickly orange streetlamps. The cityscape was still empty and an eerie silence followed us like a fog nipping at our heels.

And then, out of nowhere, I saw the first of them. It was staggering across the street, its mouth strangely agape.

"Other way!" Adam shouted and pulled me with him as we changed course.

Another one came staggering toward us, groaning quietly. Its hands lifted. Adam shoved it away and kept us running. But no matter how fast we ran, more kept appearing. They were all around us, multiplying. Their heavy groans began to fill the air in a bloodthirsty chorus.

Zombies? I thought numbly. *How…?*

"Come on!" Adam yelled, pulling me back onto an empty street.

We turned a corner and stopped dead in our tracks. A whole sea of them, like a giant, seething riot, was scrambling toward us. There was no way around. Adam pulled me to the nearest store and frantically kicked at the door. It wouldn't budge. Cursing, he threw his shoulder into it. Nothing.

Panting, he took my hand again. "We have to run," he said.

But they were all around us, moving faster. Hands raised and mouths dropped open. There were *thousands* of them.

I looked up at Adam and saw his mouth set in a grim line. "I don't understand," I said.

He pulled me close and pressed his lips to my forehead. "I'm sorry," he said. "I'm so, so sorry, Chloe."

I pressed myself to him and scrunched my eyes. They were nearly on top of us. Their groans were deafening. I screamed.

Then, above the noise, I heard something familiar. A terrible screech that pierced the air like a giant sword. I gripped Adam tighter as a great gush of flame rippled past us, throwing us against the door like a gust of burning wind. The heat was so intense I couldn't open my eyes. Beating wings pounded the air and came down in a thunderous crash. Inhuman groans bellowed as more spouts of flame turned the world a flickering yellow behind my eyelids. I squeezed Adam as tightly as I could. The screeches and groans went on and on in a mad frenzy. I peeked open an eye.

What I saw was fire. A great sea of it, stretching forever. The tall flames licked against the high buildings and filled the streets. Undead writhed in it, scrambling and collapsing. And there, in the midst of them, was Hank. He was more ferocious than I'd ever seen. His massive jaws ripped malformed bodies to ribbons while his spiked tail whipped savagely.

Then, as quickly as it began, it was over. All the groans had ceased. The only remaining sound was the roar of the flames. I slowly stood and realized Adam was gone. It was just me and

Hank now. He slowly turned, his eyes bright, and his long teeth glinting in the firelight. Tall flames surrounded us and I stepped forward. He bowed his head and I reached out to touch him, unafraid.

"Thank you," I whispered, and woke up.

THIRTY-FOUR DAYS

THE NEXT MORNING something was different. I couldn't tell how, but something was definitely off. Or not *off* necessarily, but different. I *felt* different. It was hard to put my finger on it.

With a slight shake of my head, I told myself to forget it. That was always the best technique. It's like when you can't remember a certain word. You have to stop thinking about it, and then it'll come to you.

So, returning to my usual routine, I pre-empted Chewbacca's roar and then swung my legs around to the floor. I rubbed my eyes. I stretched. I got up and found my *Star Wars* slippers.

Right as I put them on—that's when it hit me. It didn't seem possible, though, so I squinted in skepticism. I did a little hop and tested waving my arms around. I walked to and fro. I jumped onto my bed and then jumped off. I did a poor attempt at a pirouette. (I tripped and fell mid-spin, but got right back up.) I did a cartwheel. I jumped again. The evidence was really stacking up...

I looked at my hands in astonishment like I'd just developed superpowers.

Because there was no denying it. This wasn't my imagination. It was real.

I felt *better.*

And not just a little better. I felt *better,* better. Like, totally normal better. Don't ask me how, but it was the truth. I ran in a little circle to test my limbs. They worked. No aching. No dizziness. No nausea. In fact, I was actually hungry.

Right about then is when the smiling started. I couldn't stop it. I probably looked totally manic, but I didn't care. I jumped and whooped and flew down the stairs to where Mom was already making breakfast. I screeched when I entered the room, startling her into dropping a carton of eggs and she screeched back.

"Look at this," I wailed, running around the table, trailed by a freshly reinvigorated Woz.

Dad charged in a second later, still buttoning his shirt. "Are you okay?" he said. "What's going on?"

"Better, better, better!" I squealed, still running in circles. "Check this out!"

I jumped onto my palms—remembering a long lost talent from my single digit years—and did a perfect handstand in the middle of the kitchen. "Look!" I exclaimed, smiling upside down.

"Well, um, I mean…" Dad stuttered. "You look…"

"Chloe, what is going on?" Mom said, slowing stepping toward me and ignoring the eggs.

I somersaulted onto my feet and beamed. "Crazy, right?"

"That's one word for it," Dad breathed, still staring numbly.

Mom suddenly held me at arms length; her eyes darted up and down like a squirrel's. "Chloe, honey, do you really feel better?"

I shrugged. "I think so," I said. "I mean, I had this crazy dream last night and then… I don't know. I woke up this morning feeling great. I've been running around for the past ten minutes and I'm not even tired."

Suddenly Mom straightened and squared her shoulders. "We have to see Dr. Mark right away."

"That we do," I agreed. "Right after I get home from school."

She and Dad both blinked at me—shocked, incredulous, and maybe just a tad suspicious.

• • •

It took about a half hour, but I eventually convinced them. There were a lot of additional handstands, cartwheels, dance maneuvers, and finally, a game of Paper, Rock, Scissors to win them over. Before I knew it though, Mom was dropping me off in front of the school. It was just like any other day—back when days were normal. I couldn't even begin to describe how good that felt.

I headed straight for Mr. Sato's room. I'd missed it more than I'd realized. When I approached the door, I saw the usual gang huddled outside—their collective breathing puffing in the morning air. Sid had his back to me, standing next to Thu and Tad, as well as several other kids from the Chess Club.

I crept toward them, keeping my head swiveled around like I was distracted by something far away. By the time it became totally obvious that I was just hiding my face, I was already standing right behind them. With total nonchalance, I slipped into the circle, not making a sound and keeping my eyes down. It was like nothing had ever happened. Today was just another day.

My entrance was smooth and casual and completely unnoticed. At least it was unnoticed for about 0.5 seconds. Sid, of course, was the first to see me and shouted, "*What the—!*" as his jaw fell open.

All eyes instantly flipped to me and went wide as saucers.

"Hi everyone," I said, giving a little wave. I then broke into a broad smile, unable to contain it a second longer.

Shouts and jumps and questions and more shouts began in earnest, wondering "*how??*" then, "*When?*" then, "*Who cares?*"

It didn't take long before my super smile collapsed into a bout of tear-soaked laughter that threatened to melt into full-blown sobs at any moment. (Which, okay, it kind of did a couple times, but I mostly kept it in check.)

Even *Sid* started crying a little, which sparked a new round of guffaws that made everyone nearby stop and stare at us.

Once the hysteria had died down, the bell finally rang for class. Everyone said their reluctant goodbyes and made me promise to see them at lunch. All except for Sid. He didn't say a word. He just stared at me, gaping, and then—with alarming speed—gave me an enormous bear hug.

"I don't get it," he said, literally squeezing the breath out of me.

"Me neither. I'm going to the doctor after school, though. He'll know what's up."

He finally let me go and looked me over. "Chloe Freaking Cartwright," he said. "Who *are* you?"

I beamed, lifting my chin a bit. "I've been trying to keep it a secret," I said. "But the truth is: I'm a superhero. I fight crime."

"You really do," he said. "I mean… crap. I don't even know what to say."

I laughed and poked him on the chest. "That's a first."

"I can't go to class right now," he said, shaking his head. "I mean, *math?* There's no way. I'm going to class with you instead."

"Fine with me. I don't think Mr. Chamberlin will be okay with it though."

Sid bit his lip and frowned. "Yeah, you're probably right. But then again… screw it. Let's go ask him."

And so we did.

• • •

This was the last week before winter break, which meant two things: final exams and the annual "Xmas in the Quad" rally, better known as XQR. People actually went pretty nuts for it. There were giant XQR banners and posters everywhere, colored with festive greens and reds and adorned with tinsel and snowflakes and candy canes and Christmas trees and Santas and reindeer and… well, you get the picture.

And, as ironic as this might sound, XQR was more for the In Crowd than the Geek Crowd. The biggest reason was that most of the activities had taken on a somewhat... shall we say... *scandalous* quality?

The Secret Santa event—where one student would take the microphone and give a gift to another in front of the whole school—had basically devolved into a reality show entitled: "Which Good-Looking Person Likes Which Other Good-Looking Person?"

Then, of course, there was the fake snowball fight using a foam machine, which... *yeah*. You can probably guess what that one was like.

And lastly, the highlight of XQR every year was the Mistletoe Contest. It was pretty much like the Secret Santa thing, except it involved some serious PDA instead of presents. Students would submit the names of their friends who they wanted to scc kiss into a raffle box, and then the names got called by the rally's emcee, Jason Lau. Then they'd get up and kiss in front of everybody under a giant piece of mistletoe. The kisses ranged from shy little pecks, to full on make out sessions. Either way, students from my particular social strata never got called. None of us were mean/crazy enough to submit each other's names.

Still, there was no way to avoid XQR. It was held at lunch right in the middle of the quad (hence the name), and no matter where you sat, you couldn't help but watch it. I'd just joined Sid and Thu at Brick Wall Place, when the thumping, Christmas-themed rally music began.

"We gonna go watch?" Sid asked, arching an eyebrow.

"You mean like a closer view?"

"Yeah, why not?" he said, picking up his lunch bag. "It's always good for a laugh."

I shrugged and we headed over, finding a seat on the Sophomore Steps. They'd been commandeered for the rally and were packed with spectators. Absently, I noticed Dawson's

Creek sitting a little ahead of us with his friends. Thu's sudden stiffness meant that she'd definitely noticed as well. I also realized he was the only person who hadn't said "hi" to me yet. (To be fair though, I doubted he even knew I was at school. No one was really talking to him anymore.)

The rally started with great fanfare as Jason Lau took the microphone. He was our school's student body president and was very professional. And by "professional," I definitely don't mean "boring." He was like a living cartoon character. It's just that whenever he made a joke that fell completely flat—which was most of them—he moved right ahead, never skipping a beat. I was duly impressed.

The Secret Santa show began with a pair of seniors, Ally Prescott and Ben Landau, and as much as I hated to admit it, it was absurdly cute. They'd been friends for years apparently, and only now had Ben finally gotten the nerve to ask her out. His present was a giant piece of wrapping paper tightly folded inside a neat little box with a red bow on top. Once Ally opened it, he helped her unfold the paper to reveal hugely written letters, which asked, "Will You Be My Girlfriend?"

Obviously, she said yes.

She also took full advantage of the mistletoe hanging overhead.

Next up were several more pairings, but none of them were as good. Then, the last guy to go up to the stage was a ridiculously hot senior named Martin Biggs. Basically, he was the type of guy who was destined to become a male model/movie star/President of the United States—and not necessarily in that order. Anyway, when he took the mic, he produced a small, tasteful box from his pocket.

"Shucks, this is embarrassing," he admitted bashfully, although it was quite obvious there wasn't a bashful bone in his entire body. "So, there's this girl I really like and I keep chickening out every time I try to talk to her. So if public humiliation is what it takes…" He smiled at his own humility. "Emily Sulecki," he continued. "I got this for you."

I immediately winced as I glanced at Sid to my right. He seemed completely unfazed.

Emily emerged from the audience, bright red and beaming, as she strode out to greet her secret admirer. The entire school was erupting in oohs and ahs as she unwrapped the gift to find a thin, silver bracelet. Even more hoots and whistles erupted when Martin got on one knee (for some reason) and helped her put it on. He then stood and raised his arms in triumph. Everyone cheered.

I looked at Sid again and nudged him with my shoulder. "Sorry," I told him.

He shrugged. "She still likes me. You'll see."

Next up was the fake snowball fight, and despite its promise of hilarity, it was actually incredibly boring. A "red team" and a "green team" of popular seniors threw foam at each other for a few minutes until one side was declared the victor.

Yay!

Finally, the rally got to the Mistletoe Contest. I'd always secretly liked this one. I mean, it wasn't like I dreamed of getting called on stage or anything. Not at all. It was just… fun to watch. Like, it was one of those things that was super embarrassing but also super cute too. I liked that.

"Here we go!" Jason Lau boomed, dipping his hand into the raffle box. He drew out a single ticket. "Ha!" he exclaimed. "I should've guessed! Our first guy is… Adam Worley! Get up here, man!"

Oh God…

I read once that a hummingbird's heart can reach one thousand two hundred sixty beats a minute. I was currently putting that number to shame. And my mind was racing even faster. *Did someone submit my name with his?*

Didtheydidtheydidtheydidthey?? Did SID??? I bet he did, didn't he! That's why he suggested we watch!

I whirled on him, ready to attack, just as Jason Lau called out, "And the lucky lady is… surprise, surprise… his *girlfriend!* Melissa Reinhardt!"

Ooof.

Talk about conflicting emotions. Probably the world's most intense sensation of relief coupled with the world's most drooping sense of disappointment. I couldn't tell which one was bigger. (Although, to be honest, it was probably the relief.)

Melissa casually walked out to greet her boyfriend. He waited for her pleasantly, but—and I'm pretty sure I wasn't imagining this—not very excitedly either. And then, confirming that suspicion, they gave each other a simple little peck, and it was over.

I blinked in shock. What was *that?* It definitely wasn't the kiss of a happy couple. Even *I,* who's never had a proper boyfriend before, could tell.

Interesting…

"Well, that was underwhelming," Jason Lau said, frowning while his eyes followed Adam and Melissa back to their seats. "So who's next?" He reached into the raffle box again. He pulled out another ticket and smiled. "Okay," he began. "It is now my duty to summon… Joshua Travers!"

Oh boy. In case you've forgotten, "Joshua Travers" is the actual name of Dawson's Creek. And if I thought my heart had been racing a second ago, Thu's was in serious danger of going nuclear. Her whole body stiffened into a beam of steel and I was actually a little scared to be sitting next to her.

"Um…" I said cautiously. "We did *not* have anything to do with this." I looked to Sid for confirmation. "Right?"

He held up his hands. "I know nothing. I swear to Christ."

I watched dumbly as Dawson's Creek made his way up to the stage. His face was unreadable. Jason Lau then continued,

"And the girl of his dreams is… uh, hold on." He leaned over to the DJ and whispered—although the mic still totally picked it up—"Do you know who this is?"

The DJ looked at the ticket, but shook her head and shrugged.

"Anyway, sorry about that," Jason said, jumping back to face everyone. "The lucky girl is … Thu Pham!"

For some reason, I had a sudden flashback to when I first met Thu. I told you about it earlier. It was my fourth birthday party. She and I didn't even know each other's names but we started playing this game that was basically a version of hide and seek except with headbutts instead of tags. I could still remember it clearly. She had a very hard head. I just hoped she wasn't planning on using it on me now.

An odd silence had blanketed the quad. Plenty of students were probably wondering, "Who's Thu Pham?" until—quite abruptly—they got their answer.

She stood up straight, stone-faced, and started making her way down the crowded steps. I shared a slow glance with Sid. Neither of us could believe it. Why was she going down there? She didn't have to. She could've fled. Yet there she was, only steps away from Dawson's Creek in front of the entire school. Was she going to headbutt him?

They stared at each other for an eternity. Dawson's Creek's face remained impassive, while Thu's was grim. She stood with her arms locked at her sides and her fists balled. I was all but positive she was about to attack. The silence deepened. There was hardly a butt in the whole quad that wasn't on the edge of its step.

Then it happened.

Thu took a small step forward. Dawson's Creek took a small step forward. Their eyes remained pinned. No one dared to breathe. A few more seconds passed until finally a single, solitary voice rose from the crowd and shouted, "Make out already!"

And they did.

They *really* did.

Thu pounced on him and he fell onto his back. It didn't stop her. She kissed him and he kissed her, and they literally rolled in the grass like lovers separated by a war.

Everyone broke into a standing ovation and my astonishment quickly became laughter. I stood and clapped. Sid hugged me again. His eyes shone with a brilliant, "I told you so!"

Task #1—Get Thu and Dawson's Creek back together—had just been accomplished. I couldn't understand how, but it had. All on its own.

"Awesome, right?" a small voice said.

Sid released me and I found his little sister Piya standing beside me. She wore a wide, triumphant smile. "I'm so good at math, it's scary," she noted.

I paused and squinted at her. "What do you mean?" I asked slowly.

"I stuffed the ballots," she stated proudly. "In a smart way."

No way...

"A smart way?" I said.

"Yep. I used a regression analysis to calculate an average of fifty tickets in the total raffle—which is actually really complicated. Then I added precisely fifty more tickets for Joshua Travers and Thu Pham. Get it?"

"No."

"Well, that way, they would have a *roughly* fifty percent chance three times in a row. However, due to probability theory, there was only a twelve percent chance of their ticket being drawn all three times, thus drawing suspicion. I just want to see who the final ticket is for. There's a forty-nine percent chance it'll be for Joshua and Thu again, but there's only a twelve percent chance of that. Cool, right?"

I stared blankly. "I... I mean... *when?*"

Piya shrugged. "Sid told me it didn't work out at the restaurant. I figured this might work better. I did good, right?"

Good? I thought. *Good?????*

Without another word, I jumped on her. She giggled happily while Sid made a face. I couldn't believe it. Piya had stuffed the ballots? Piya the Mathlete??

And Thu and Dawson's Creek were still kissing!! Talk about PDA... Even Jason Lau was turning red. I burst into laughter again, albeit this time with tears.

Task #1 = Accomplished.

Perhaps The Plan wasn't dead after all.

It lived on.

THIRTY-THREE DAYS

THE NEXT DAY in Physics was our "Fun Final." (The real final was tomorrow. I planned on taking it just for fun.) The Fun Final, in case you forgot, was our assignment to find an interesting TED Talk and do a quick presentation on it. I'd decided weeks ago to do mine on this one lecture about quantum physics. It was pretty complicated stuff, but I had a complex stratagem for making it simpler. It involved a certain boy named…

"Adam," I said before the bell rang. He turned to me, looking up from a note card with his speech on it.

"Chloe."

"Can I have your phone number?"

He grinned and slid over his phone with the number cued up. I called it and saved the name.

"Thanks."

A second later the bell rang and Mr. Bowen bounced in front of the class. "Okay," he said hurriedly. "We have twenty-four presentations and fifty-six minutes to do them. Who wants to go first?"

My hand instantly shot up.

I have no idea *why* it did this. I had no desire to go first, and yet there it was—straining like it wanted to touch the ceiling.

"Excellent," Mr. Bowen said. "Miss Cartwright. I've been looking forward to this one."

I blushed at that. Or more accurately, I blushed *more.* I mean, in the past thirty seconds, I'd asked Adam Worley for his phone number and volunteered to speak in front of our whole class. What was next? A surprise visit from Zac Efron?

I shuddered.

"Okay," I said, making my way up to the front of the room. "My topic's kind of weird, so I'll do my best."

"Weird is good." Mr. Bowen nodded. "And remember. This doesn't count toward your grade. Just have fun."

I swallowed as I turned to face everyone. My stomach was starting to tighten against a rising panic. "Um, okay," I said again. "So, here it is. My name is Chloe Cartwright and I am a quantum particle."

There was a murmur of confused laughter at that. I felt my cheeks go even redder. (If that was possible.)

"Er... what I mean by that is... okay. So there are like two separate types of physics. There's regular physics and there's quantum physics. The regular physics is for big stuff, like you and me, and all the normal-sized things in this room. Quantum physics is for all the really small stuff, like atoms and electrons and quarks."

I looked to Mr. Bowen who seemed imminently pleased as he nodded in encouragement.

"Yeah," I said. "So in quantum physics, tiny particles—otherwise known as 'fundamental particles'—behave by totally different rules. They can walk through walls, they can be in two places at once, and they can teleport across the entire universe in a blink. Basically, they can do all sorts of things that don't make any sense and *should* be completely impossible. But they do them anyway. So I guess the question is: Why am *I* a quantum particle?"

I briefly looked around the room, but no one raised their hand. They *did* seem interested though. (Maybe?)

"Well," I said. "I suppose the idea is that maybe there *aren't* two types of physics after all. Maybe big things go by the same rules as particles and we just don't realize it. Because if big things are entirely made of small things, then shouldn't they follow the same rules? Well, that's what some really smart physicists tried to figure out. They did this experiment where they created a really tiny piece of silicon that was still visible to the naked eye and made it behave as if it were a quantum particle. I don't fully understand *how* they did it, but it had something to do with putting the silicon into a complete vacuum. The point is, they *did* it. The tiny piece of metal started vibrating, and also *not vibrating* at the same time. Basically it, and all of its trillions of atoms, were in two places at once."

I stopped again to see if everyone was still listening. My eyes settled on Adam for a brief second and he smiled.

"So the last thing," I continued. "And this is really the coolest part, is that the difference in scale between the little chunk of metal and a single atom is about the same as the difference in size between the little chunk of metal and you. So then if one atom can be in two places at once, and the little piece of metal can be in two places at once, then so can *you*. And to demonstrate this…" I paused, thumbing at my phone inside my pocket. A couple seconds later, someone else's phone rang.

Adam Worley answered. "Hello?" he said.

I looked right at him and smiled. "Hi," I said. Our eyes locked for a second longer than necessary and my stomach started doing somersaults again. I quickly glanced away, determined to finish.

"So," I said importantly. "There's the proof. I'm both here and there. Two places at once. And when you think about how tiny I am compared to the entire universe with all its billions of galaxies and stuff, then... yeah. My name is Chloe Cartwright, and I am a quantum particle."

With that, Mr. Bowen bolted out of his chair and began clapping like a madman. "YES!" he exclaimed. "That's what I'm talking about! Physics!"

The rest of the class followed suit and I crumpled into a pile of embarrassed giggles, making a hasty retreat to my seat.

"Wow." Adam raised an eyebrow at me. "I pity the fool who has to follow *that.*"

I buried my face in my palms. "I am so embarrassed right now."

"Well," he said casually. "At least I have your phone number now."

Yeah. Er... wait. What?

Slowly, I peeked through my fingers at him.

"What?" he said innocently.

THIRTY DAYS

THINGS WERE LOOKING UP. Dr. Mark had told me my labs had rebounded. Final exams were over. (I breezed right through them and, considering that I hadn't studied at all, probably didn't do half bad.) Also, there was the thing about Adam Worley apparently wanting my number? And most of all—Thu and Dawson's Creek were a couple again. And not just a secret couple like last time. They were a very, very, *very* public couple.

Anyway, their reunion was awesome for several reasons, the most important of which was: "Friday Night? Game Night!"

That's right. Dungeons & Dragons was back. My house. Me. Sid. Thu. Dawson's Creek. And now, three new members. Tad, his girlfriend Jen, and—much to Sid's dismay—Piya. Of course, all three of them were total noobs, but still. Our gang of four was now a gang of seven.

Sid tapped his pencil/gavel on the kitchen table and stood like he was about to give a speech. Several Cheetos were thrown at him.

"I call this campaign to order," he announced solemnly. He then paused, looking around the table. "I see some new faces," he added, sounding more and more like a wizard. "And I see some old. Such is the way of the Multiverse. The important thing is that we're all here together—united in a single purpose. A *fellowship,* if you will."

"Dear god," Dawson's Creek groaned, massaging his eyes. "Really? Lord of the Rings?"

Sid blanched. "I know not of what you speak, noble Pacey. I merely wish to inaugurate this—"

"Fellowship of the Ring?" I asked.

He frowned. "All right fine," he said, dropping the Gandalf voice. "Perhaps 'fellowship' was the wrong word. I do, however, want to say welcome back"—he pointed to Thu and Dawson's Creek who were cuddled together and... um, *snuggling*—"to these two ridiculous people. Their prolonged absence totally screwed up our last campaign, but we will hold no grudges. I'd also like to call for an immediate vote on 'No Public Displays of Affection' during gameplay. All in favor?"

No one raised their hand. Or, well, Sid did. But no one else.

"Damn," he muttered.

Thu grinned happily at him.

"Anyway," he continued. "As Dungeon Master, I also wanted to welcome our newcomers. Tad. Jen. It's great to have you here."

Piya scowled at him. "I'm here too, loser."

Sid continued without acknowledging her. "I've always wanted the *two* of you to join, and I'm sure we'll all have a lot of fun. I believe Chloe has volunteered to help you learn the rules?"

I nodded happily.

"Excellent. So without further ado—"

Piya's hand shot up in earnest. "Is it true that Adam Worley likes Chloe?" she asked.

I suddenly blushed. "*What?*"

She continued speaking in a single breath. "My friend Amy from the Denominators is in your Physics class and *she* said that—"

"Dungeons!" Sid cut in. "Dragons! And you two!" He stabbed an accusatory finger at Tad and Jen. "No making out at the table!"

"Sorry," they both said sheepishly.

Piya talked right over him. "Don't listen to him," she said. "He's just mad about Emily and that Martin guy. He's *so* hot…"

Sid groaned and let his forehead smack into the table. "I need more *dude* friends," he groaned.

"Okay," I said. "It's D&D time. Shall we?"

"We shall," Dawson's Creek and Thu said in unison. Then Thu added, "Sid, you're the Dungeon Master. Stop stalling, let's go!"

Everyone laughed as he raised his head to toss her a weary look. "Yes," he said. "The Lost Freaking Key. Let's do this."

And so Dungeons & Dragons began. Dice were rolled. Rules were allegedly broken. Arguments ensued. I loved every second of it.

It had been four months since our last game together. A lot of things had happened in that time. Relationships. Plans. School Plays. Crushes. Everywhere Cancer. Some of these things had yet to reach their conclusion, but the ones that had were good. Thu and Dawson's Creek were back together. Sid was in love—though he'd never admit it. Tad and Jen were a couple. Adam Worley might like me…

They say that the past is prologue, but I doubt my situation is quite what "they" had in mind. Still, yesterday was a good day, and so was today. Sid, Thu, Dawson's Creek. We were gathered around my kitchen table once more. Cheetos. Mountain Dew. Friends, in each other's company.

TWENTY-THREE DAYS

WE'D AGREED TO KEEP Christmas low key this year. It was just me, Mom, Dad and Henry. I liked it better that way. Usually, boatloads of relatives came over, which wasn't horrible or anything, but was also pretty chaotic. There was never enough time to really *talk* to anyone. It all just became a big blur of Christmas music and gingerbread men. This time, though, things were calm. No pressure. No big dinners with tons of dishes. No last minute shopping. No piles of presents under the tree. This time it was just one present each. (Plus stockings, of course.)

And you know what? I'm gonna go ahead and keep a little secret from you. I mean, *something* has to be for me, and just me, right? You don't need to know *everything*. So… yeah. I'm gonna skip telling you what my parents got me. What I *will* say is that it was very, very cool, and made me laugh and cry at the same time.

Perhaps you'd like to guess what it was? Maybe?

Ah, you'll never get it.

Anyway, it was my sixteenth Christmas, and while I didn't have the best recollection of the first few—the ones where I was Henry's age—I decided that this one was my very favorite. It was warm and cozy, and simple and good. We sifted through stockings. Exchanged presents. Ate pancakes. Watched Christmas movies. And when it was time to go to bed, we kissed each other good night and said, "I love you."

Sometimes those three little words are automatic. Other times they are truly felt. I'll let you guess as to which of those times this was.

TWENTY DAYS

I WAS WORKING ON Henry's letter in my room when Dad appeared in the doorway with his laptop and a guilty look.

"Can I come in?" he asked, knocking on the frame.

I turned in my seat and raised my nose a bit. "You *may*," I said with a small smile.

He smiled back and stepped in, sitting on the edge of my bed.

"I wasn't snooping," he said quickly. "I really wasn't. It's just that I bought that multi-pack last year and now everyone's looks the same and it's a mess. Plus, now that I think about it, I probably should've labeled mine. I mean, jeez, if the one I use for work got into the wrong hands I could get in serious—"

"Dad," I interrupted. "I have *no* idea what you're talking about right now."

He grinned sheepishly. "I ramble at times," he admitted. "The important thing is that I wasn't snooping. I wanted you to know that before I came clean."

"Came clean?" I asked.

He drew a breath. "Well, the thing is… last night I was looking for one of my flash drives and I couldn't find it anywhere. Eventually my search led me to your room and…"

He kept going but I wasn't listening anymore. I knew exactly where this was going. My heart started pounding. He'd found *the* flash drive. The one with the movie I'd made with seminal family moments. The one from The Plan. *Oh crap, oh crap, oh crap, oh…*

178

WHERE THE DRAGONS GO

"Chloe?" he said.

I perked up, trying to appear as though I'd been listening. "Hmm?"

"Sweetheart, did you make this?"

He had flipped his laptop around to show me the screen. I felt a pang in my stomach and chewed my lip in embarrassment.

Yes, I did make that, I thought, nodding slightly. *Just please, please, please don't ask me why...*

"Why?" he asked.

Really??

"Um." I squirmed. "I, uh…"

I suddenly felt so stupid I could cry. It was strange. I *shouldn't* have felt stupid, but I did. Seeing the movie cued up on his laptop like this, in the middle of the afternoon, made the whole Plan seem so childish. What did I think was going to happen? I'd show them a home movie and then everything would be better? *Stupid, stupid, stupid, stu...*

"Chloe," he interrupted again. "I'm not upset, honey. Gosh, why would I be? It's just… well, I guess I just wanted to know. That's all."

I couldn't even look him in the eye. And yet he was looking at me so inquisitively I wanted to burst. A rush of tears was building up like water behind a dam. My lip quivered as I attempted to look up.

"I…" I started to say, but my throat tightened. It was like the size of what I wanted to say was too big. All the tumult of the past few months—The Plan, dying, parents, friends, dragons, love, loss and all the things I'd never get to see… It all came crowding over me, spinning like a carousel of unlived memories. I didn't want to go. I didn't want to leave. And now my dad was looking at me with his big curious eyes, showing me a shattered piece of The Plan—the one thing I'd meant to leave behind. It was too much. I couldn't hold it in. He put a hand on my shoulder and the dam burst.

"I had a plan!" I cried, burying my face in my palms as my shoulders heaved with heavy sobs. He shot forward and took me in his arms. "Sweetheart," he said. "It's okay, it's okay!"

"It's not okay!"

I wanted to explain more, but the tears kept coming. Dad squeezed me tighter and stroked my hair, whispering, "It'll be all right. Do you hear me? It will be all right."

"I'm sorry," I finally croaked though gasping breaths. "I'm so sorry, Dad."

He kept stroking my hair. "There's nothing to be sorry for, sweetheart. Do you understand? Nothing."

"I wanted to make things better," I tried to explain. "I had this big plan to... I don't know. It just fell apart."

"I understand," he said. "It's okay."

I kept crying for a while longer. Dad stayed with me, awkwardly kneeling in front of my chair to hug me. When the tears finally slowed, I did my best to compose myself. I wiped my face, blew my nose and tried to sit upright.

With a final sniffle, I told him I was okay and he reluctantly returned to his seat on the edge of my bed.

After a moment, he said, "I didn't mean to upset you."

The words kind of hung in the air a moment as we both looked at each other. Me—a blubbering mess. Him—covered in my snot.

I cracked a small smile and he did the same. Then, as if reading each other's minds, we both burst into laughter.

"Yeah," I said. "Well done!"

"Sorry," he replied.

We laughed some more and he said, "So..."

I looked at him. "So?"

"So... I thought the movie was really good?"

"Thanks," I chuckled, wiping my eyes again. "It took me a month. Sorry about pilfering all your movie files."

He shrugged. "My life's an open book. Feel free to pilfer any time."

"Nothing incriminating," I said.

"Ha!" he snorted.

Another pause drifted between us. Eventually I winced, as I figured I should just come clean with the whole truth.

"So it was a couple months ago," I began. "Sid was in on it, and some of my other friends too. We called it 'The Plan.' Pretty original, right?"

He nodded and I proceeded to explain everything that happened. I told him about my plans for Sid, Dr. Mark, Thu, and of course, for him and Mom. He started apologizing profusely when I got to the part about him staying late at work, but I assured him it was fine. Then, once everything was out in the open, he stared at me a long while.

"You know what?" he finally said.

"What?"

"Your plan wasn't a bad idea." He rubbed his chin and looked down in thought. The wheels were clearly turning. And when my dad's wheels turned, they *really* turned. He designed computer games for a living. Like, *cool* games too. Have I mentioned that before? Anyway. Definitely not a profession for the dull-witted.

"I'm starting to get an idea here," he said slowly. Then, like lightning, he snapped his fingers and his eyes shot up. "Yes," he said seriously. "A big idea. A big idea indeed. And you, daughter mine, are going to help me."

SEVENTEEN DAYS

"WAIT. YOU WERE WEARING A *WHAT*?" I asked as I rode on the back of our shopping cart through the isles of Target.

"A gorilla suit," Dad answered matter of factly. "Not the best outfit to go jogging in, believe me." He peered down at his shopping list and frowned. "Where do you think they sell the tablecloths? I'm looking for one of those Italian-style ones. Like red and white checkered, you know?"

"Maybe over there?" I pointed.

He followed my finger and grinned. "Good eye, kid. Let's do this."

We headed over to Home Furnishings and I grilled him some more about how he first met Mom.

"I was only twenty back then," he said. "We were both at Cal and running in the Bay to Breakers—you know that big race in the city?"

I nodded.

"It's totally nuts," he explained. "Like a hundred thousand people run in it every year wearing crazy costumes. I'd decided to do it in a gorilla suit. Which actually—"

"Why?"

He looked down at me and lifted his eyebrows. "Because I'm an idiot. I also didn't realize how hot it would get in that thing. Nevertheless, I *would've* made it to the finish line if it weren't for your mom."

"But you didn't know her yet, right?"

"No. But my God. When I first saw her, it wasn't even a choice. I *had* to meet her. She was too beautiful not to try."

"Where was she?"

"Well, she was running in the race and she passed me. I was jogging with some friends when she zipped by. Very fast, your mother. Legs like a gazelle."

I paused a moment as I tried to get a mental picture. If she ran past him then—

"So…" I said slowly. "What you're saying—and for the record: *Ew*—is that you saw her butt? Am I understanding this correctly?"

He pursed his lips and squinted. "*Hmm*. Well she was jogging with her friend and kept turning so there was a bit of a side profile as well, but…"

"Wow," I finished.

He chuckled awkwardly. "So. Moving on. I, uh, *saw her*. And then I decided to catch her by any means necessary."

"Double ew."

"Yes. Only the problem was that I was wearing that darn gorilla suit. It was like a hundred and fifty degrees in there. Plus, and I'm not sure if you've noticed this, but your mother tends to be in pretty good shape. And I'm, well… *not*."

I giggled. "I've noticed."

"So I started sprinting. And even then, it took about a minute to catch up. My friends were shouting at me like I'd gone insane. Once I was finally running alongside her, I was so out of breath I could barely think."

I pointed ahead. "I think those are the tablecloths," I said.

"Ah. Perfect."

"So what happened next?"

He drew a long breath, as if remembering something particularly embarrassing. "Well," he exhaled. "I did the best I could."

"The best you could?"

"Pick up line-wise."

I laughed and then gaped at him. "I don't think I even want to know. But... okay, I do. Tell me, tell me, tell me."

He looked past me, distracted. "Really honey, it's been so many years. I honestly don't remember."

"Just tell me!"

He stopped to examine some fabric. "You think this one looks good?"

"Dad."

He turned. "Yes?"

I stared at him, making my eyes as big as possible. After a desperate moment, he caved.

"Okay fine," he huffed. "I said to her—and bear in mind I was panting heavily behind a mask so it might have come out muffled—but I said: 'Excuse me. Are you a fan of Dr. Seuss? Because green eggs and... damn!'"

There was a long, fat silence as I took a moment for the horrendousness of this pick up line to sink in. I mean... *Dr. Seuss?* It was almost borderline *creepy.*

Eventually, I made a sour face and said, "Um...wow. Green Eggs and Ham. Nice one, Dad."

He shrugged, deciding on one of the tablecloths and tossing it in the cart. "She didn't get it either. We need candles now."

I pointed. "Over there, I think. So what happened next? Don't tell me she fell for it?"

"She didn't."

"So?"

"So she gave me a look—kind of like the one you're giving me right now—and started running faster. Then, smart guy that I was, I sprinted even harder to keep up. That lasted for about, I don't know, ten, twenty seconds until I tripped over my own feet and went flying. I've been told that as far as 'tumbles' go, it was pretty epic—you know, with my legs flying up over my head and such. I also blacked out for a second or two. Anyway, the next thing I knew, a pair of hands was lifting the gorilla mask off my head, and there was your mom."

"What did she say?"

He chuckled. "Well, this is where accounts differ. Your mom insists that she called me an idiot—but in a good way. Know what I mean?"

I nodded.

"*I*, on the other hand," he said, "remember her saying, '*Oh. You're actually kinda cute...*'"

"That's more romantic," I said.

"It is. But I easily could've imagined it. All I know is that she was smiling. I'll never forget that part. Ah, here we go." He stopped in front of a large wall of candles.

"She'll like these ones," I said, picking some long, skinny ones out of a tray.

He nodded. "Great minds think alike."

"So what's next?" I asked.

"Cheap collapsible tables," he said. "Where do you think—?"

"Home and Garden," I answered, and we started heading in that direction. After a bit, I looked up at him, as he once again squinted down at his shopping list.

"Dad," I said. "I'm actually really impressed. I mean, your attempt was horrible and everything, but you *did* it. And it worked."

He shrugged again, but smiled. "We all have our moments. Speaking of which, we better hurry. We still have to beat the traffic and then stop at Papa John's."

So we hurried. And as we picked up our last supplies for The Plan 2.0, I realized something important. Dad's goofy story about how he met Mom was basically the very first page of *my* story. That day, with him in a gorilla suit and her taking pity on him, was when I began. I wouldn't exist if he hadn't had the courage to chase after her, nor would I exist if she hadn't been nice enough to stop and help him. There are plenty of people who wouldn't have done either. So I guess in a way, they were both sort of *superheroes* that day. Not because of me. I'm not saying that. I'm just saying that the ingredients were there. A dash of bravery. A pinch of kindness. And that's how the world gets saved, one person at a time.

Oh yeah. That was definitely going in Henry's letter.

• • •

If there was one thing Dad knew, it was the art of the Grand Gesture. It was New Year's Eve, a little before eleven, and we were setting up shop along the waterfront of San Francisco's Embarcadero. According to him, we were in the exact place were he'd tripped and first met Mom. It was a nice spot, right along the shoreline. The water was oily black, and glittered with the lights of the surrounding city.

I was on lookout duty—both for Mom... *and for the cops*—as Dad made his final preparations. He'd set up a small table, complete with Italian-ish tablecloth, two candles and a large pepperoni pizza right off the main walkway. A couple hours earlier, he'd texted Mom to meet him about a mile away. (Henry was with a babysitter.) The plan was for her to find a clue, kind of like a treasure hunt, and then find another and another, until she happened upon us. By Dad's calculations, she was due to arrive at any moment.

"Anything?" he called out to me.

I lowered my binoculars and turned. "Not yet," I said.

"Okay, good." He kneeled on the grass and unzipped a large duffle bag. At first, I couldn't tell what he was pulling out of it until I realized aloud, "Is that the *gorilla suit?*"

"It is," he called back. "When your mother arrives, she'll see the table but I won't be in sight. I'm gonna hide behind that tree over there and scare the bejesus out of her."

I winced. "Dad, are you sure that's a good idea?"

"Positive. Just shout when you see her."

Turning back around, I raised the binoculars. As if on cue, I saw her walking briskly—still in her gym clothes—up the path. She was getting steadily closer and I estimated she'd reach us in a couple minutes.

I trotted back to the table. "She's coming," I hissed. (I didn't need to whisper, of course, but there was something about the moment that made me do it anyway.)

He finished wiggling himself into the long, hairy legs. "Crap," he muttered. "Okay take the pizza and go hide. Don't bring it until I give you the thumbs up."

"On it," I said, and ran off with the box. I ducked behind a parked car and peeked over the hood. I had a good view.

A minute later, Mom came wandering up to the table. She stopped and picked up the final clue. It was a note and her face looked intensely quizzical as she read it. Whatever it said, it was apparently long. She stood there reading it for at least a full minute. Meantime, I watched with bated breath as a shadowy gorilla figure crept up behind her. I couldn't help but guess at how she'd react. Would she recognize him? Would she remember this was how they first met? Would she laugh? (It would've been really nice to hear her laugh again.)

Dad was only two feet behind her now. His hands rose toward her throat. Then, quick as a gunshot, a loud shriek pierced the air. I gasped as the movements came in a blur. Mom had clearly forgotten all of her judo-style defense training. Instead, she opted for an Indiana Jones face punch and a mid-waist tackle. The next thing I knew they were both on the ground, rolling perilously close to the table.

Then, as quickly as it began, it stopped. Mom had him pinned, but wasn't attacking anymore. The gorilla mask had been torn off and Dad was laughing hysterically. No Mom laughter, though. Not yet. They remained motionless for a moment, talking in low voices. Mom's back was too me so I couldn't tell what was happening. Was this a happy conversation or an angry one?

Then I heard it. Mom laughter. And it was different than her usual laugh. It was younger somehow, more girly. Like a giggle fit. And with that, I saw a single, hairy paw rise in the air, giving me the thumbs up.

I jumped from my hiding spot and skipped over with the pizza. When I arrived Mom tried to narrow her eyes at me but couldn't hold it. "You were in on this, you traitor?" she asked.

"The gorilla costume was new," I said. "I cautioned against it. Pizza?"

She stood, helping Dad up, and moved her nose toward the box in one swift motion. "Sweet Jesus," she whispered reverently. "Is that pepperoni?"

I scrunched my nose a little in confusion. "Um... yeah?" I said.

"Told you," Dad said. "Papa John's is this woman's kryptonite. Don't let the kale chips fool you. She loves junk food more than the rest of us combined."

After that, we moved over to the table. The pizza was distributed on paper plates, soft drinks were poured, and the two cheap candles from Target were lit. And sitting there along the water's edge, with occasional passersby waving hello, it was like a little slice of heaven. (No pun intended.) We talked and joked, and did our best to keep our plates from blowing away. The wind was chilly, rolling in off the bay. I briefly put on Dad's gorilla mask for warmth.

Once we were done, (Mom *devoured* the pizza, by the way), Dad cautioned that we should pack up the table before we got in trouble. We'd been there an hour, and it was nearly midnight. I set to work packing up the tablecloth and then ran the plates over to a garbage bin. Right when I got there a sudden burst lit up the sky. It was bright white and a loud *boom* echoed across the bay.

Fireworks. I beamed up at them, lost in the spectacle. Reds and whites and blues and yellows sparkled down and glittered skyward, reflecting off the water. It was officially a new year. Part of me couldn't quite believe it. I'd made it. I'd actually made it. And standing there, staring up at the bright colors, I realized that this was one of those *moments* in life. They come along every once in a while, they never last long, and they're as fragile as glass. But when they come, you know it, because everything is clearer, simpler. Suddenly, the world isn't complicated at all. It's just here and now, and nothing else. All the things you've ever worried about don't actually exist. Life— in spite of all the bad—is *good.*

And then you look over and see your parents making out and… oh. *Ew. Double ew!* But… good. I guess. Eyes back to the fireworks.

I watched a while longer, giving them some space. It then occurred to me that The Plan 2.0 wasn't a 2.0 at all. It was just the original—succeeding late. Thu and Dawson's Creek were together. Mom and Dad were kissing. I was kicking butt with Henry's letter. Dr. Mark and Miss Collins… well, they were still a toss up. There wasn't much I could do for them at this point. Which was probably for the best. It was foolish of me to meddle in the affairs of doctors and teachers anyway. They'd figure things out themselves.

So, yeah. The Plan was almost complete. The only person left was…

THIRTEEN DAYS

SID CAME BOUNDING UP to me at lunch on our first day back at school. He was smiling hugely.

"Hey Chloe," he said.

"Hey Sid."

"Having a good day?" he asked.

"I guess. You?"

"The weather sure is nice. Really sunny."

I nodded. "Yeah, it's warm."

"So. Next week, huh?"

"Next week?" I asked.

"It's a big week."

"Um... *why?*"

His smile got even bigger, which I wouldn't have thought possible. "No reason," he said with a shrug and left me standing there scratching my head as he strode over to Brick Wall Place. His pace was slow and casual. He even started *whistling*.

After a moment, I trotted after him. "Okay, what is it?" I asked.

"Huh?"

"What's next week?"

"Oh. Nothing."

"It has to be *something*."

He halted, looking suddenly pensive. "You know," he said, putting an arm around my shoulder. "I seem to recall a certain exchange of texts a while back. An exchange of texts in which *you* thought I was crazy. Do you remember that?"

I frowned. "I think you're going to have to be more specific," I said, although I already had a strong suspicion of what he was talking about. In fact, once I thought about it, I knew *exactly* where he was going with this. It was written all over his face.

"Emily Sulecki," he said matter of factly. "A lovely lass… Long fiery hair. Bright blue eyes. Incredible boobs. Remember her?"

"You had to mention the boobs, didn't you?" I said. "Couldn't have just said something about her smile?"

"I save the best for last. Anyway, guess who came up to me between classes today?"

"Um. Emily?"

He squinted a moment in thought. "Hmm," he said. "I suppose that would be the obvious answer. Perhaps I played that wrong. Still!" He brightened, standing a little straighter. "She came up to me between first and second period. I was walking with Tad—who can independently verify all of this—when she came up behind me and whacked me on the shoulder."

"You mean, like, punched you?" I asked.

He shook his head. "I believe her intention was to *tap* me on the shoulder, but as I explained to you before… all that pent up desire."

I rolled my eyes.

He continued, "So I turned and she just stood there, staring at me. She had this intense sort of scowl, like she was furious with herself. I said, 'can I help you?' and she just fidgeted. Then Tad said, 'uh, what's going on?' and I said, 'I don't know,' and then Emily said, 'Sid!' and I said, 'yeah?' and she said, like really angrily, '*Will you go to the stupid Sadies Dance with me??*'"

I suddenly stopped, turned slowly, and gaped at him. His giant smile returned.

A Sadie Hawkins dance, in case you don't know, is that one dance a year where the girls get to turn the tables on the boys, and ask *them* to go, instead of the other way around. It's a chance for them to see how *they* enjoy the agony of waiting and waiting and...

"Wait," I said. "You're being serious right now, right? You're not just messing with me?"

He looked injured. "Would I joke about something like this?"

I considered that for a moment, and then concluded, "Yes."

"I would," he agreed. "But I'm not. The poor girl fought it as best she could. But in the end, she couldn't help herself."

I honestly didn't know what to say. I just stared at him. I mean, I'd always wanted this to happen, and it was definitely my intent when I Much Adoed About Nothing the two of them a couple months ago in Drama class, but still... I couldn't quite believe it. I'd totally thought my plan had backfired and they hated each other. Or at least, that Emily hated Sid. I doubted Sid was capable of hating anybody.

I felt a sudden need to hug him, but just as I moved to do so, something terrifying occurred to me.

"Um, you did say 'yes,' right?" I asked.

He looked at me, serious, and answered flatly, "No."

Of course he hadn't. That would've been too easy. He was going to play some sort of weird mind game with the poor girl now. I just knew it. Why did he have to make everything so difficult?? The Plan had almost succeeded!

"Only a fool would've simply said 'yes,'" he explained. "I'm not a robot. I'm a human being. I said to her, 'you bet your incredible ass I will!' Now admittedly, her face kind of contorted into a grimace when I said that, but she kinda smiled too. So I guess it's all goo—"

He didn't get to finish his sentence because I was already hugging him. "Are you kidding me??" I squealed.

"Me and Emily," he said. "Next Friday. And I have a bit of news for *you* as well, Chloe Cartwright."

I released him. "Me?" I asked.

He nodded. "I just heard that your lacrosse-playing super crush broke up with his girlfriend over break."

I slowly backed away. I knew this would happen. Ever since that stupid Mistletoe contest. My heart pounded. Sid was going to force me to do something—talk to him or worse. Like in the middle of the quad. I'd been dreading this moment for as along as I could remember.

With as much strength as I could muster, I chirped, "So?"

Sid frowned. "What do you mean, 'so?' So, you're asking that dude to the dance. That's what's so."

"No, I'm not."

"Yes, you are."

I backed away some more. "No, I'm not."

He then smiled lazily and shrugged. "That's cool," he said. "He's right over there." He pointed blatantly. "I'll go ask him for you. Don't worry about it."

"No!" I pounced on him again. It was like déjà vu. I remembered Thu jumping on him at the start of the year for a very similar reason. Now, due to my own stupid scheming, it was me.

TWELVE DAYS

So now it was Physics and Adam Worley was sitting five inches away. I mean, he was just *sitting* there. Oblivious. Carefree. Leaning over and chatting with his friend Brian. I watched with only my eyes, not moving my head. My heart raced, yet I was still as a statue.

Did I recently say something about how much nicer it must be to be the asker instead of the askee?

Yeah. Nevermind about that.

Sadies *sucks*.

But I had to do this. I couldn't chicken out, even if that was my gigantically overwhelming preference. Sid was a crazy person. If I didn't ask Adam by next Monday (exactly six days from now), Sid *would* do it for me. There was no question. He'd probably drag me along and... I shuddered to even imagine it.

But enough about that. What was I going to say? How was I going to ask? The words were tricky. I couldn't just *ask* him. What if I jumbled things up mid-sentence? How would I recover? I needed a plan. I needed to come up with a solid proposal and then memorize the crap out of it. I ran through some options:

Hey Adam, would you like to go to the Sadies dance with me next week?

Good. But too formal. I needed to loosen it up. Plus, was it specific enough? Should I say next "Friday" instead of next "week?" Let's try again:

> *Hey Adam, if you're going to the Sadies dance next Friday, do you think you might consider me to go with?*

Hmm. That was worse, wasn't it?

> *Hey Adam, I'd like to ask if you know about the Sadies dance next week, which falls on a Friday, and if you'd like to go to it? With me?*

Yikes…

> *Hey Adam, I heard that you might be going to the dance next week, and I thought that if you were, then maybe I could be the one who asks you to go to it?*

OMG.

> *Adam. I'd like to inquire as to your thoughts on the Sadie Hawkins dance next Friday, January 15th and if you were planning to go, and if so, I'd like to be the one that you go with.*

Okay, new plan. Simplicity. You can do this!

> *So Adam, what are you doing next January 15th, which is a Friday? Because I was told there is a Sadies dance occurring, and I was wondering if you were going, and if you were going to do so, then I'd like to be the one you consider to go with?*

That settled it. I wasn't doing it today. I was going home, I was coming up with a good line, I was writing it down, I was memorizing it, and then, once fully prepared, I was asking Adam Worley *tomorrow*.

ELEVEN DAYS

YOU KNOW WHAT? I figured out the problem. I'd been trying to ask everything all at once. Like in one single question convey the idea that there was a Sadie Hawkins dance next Friday and that I wanted to know if Adam Worley wanted to go to it. With me.

That was my folly. Too much in one question. The solution was this:

Me: So Adam, are you going to the Sadies dance next Friday?

Adam: Nope.

Me: Oh. Do you want to go with me?

Adam: Sure.

See? Isn't that better? Now all I had to do was get it started. Just one simple question with an equally simple follow up. That's all it was. I could do this. He was right there. Five inches away. And not talking to Brian. Was he waiting for me? Maybe?

Just turn to him and say it. Just turn to him and say it. Just turn to him and say it. Just turn to him and say it. Just turn to him and say it.

I then learned that within fifty-six minutes, a human being can repeat the phrase "just turn to him and say it," approximately 3,362 times.

So. Tomorrow?

TEN DAYS

YEP. I chickened out again.

NINE DAYS

And again.

SIX DAYS

OKAY, SO TODAY WAS MY LAST CHANCE. According to Sid, however, that meant the deadline had already passed. I literally had to wrestle him to the ground during lunch to stop him. So he gave me one more try. I had to do it in class today.

Or else.

And so there I sat, wondering: *Should I do it before the bell rings? Like, right now? Just get it over with? Or should I wait? Maybe after class?*

The options tumbled around in my head like a laundry machine. I had one minute, seventeen seconds left before class started. I mean, he was just sitting there, and I was just sitting there, and it was actually getting a little awkward that we weren't talking, so...

I turned to him stiffly and he nodded. "Sup?" he said.

My head sprang back into position, eyes locked straight ahead. "Hey," I chirped.

Do it, Chloe! Just do it!

"So Adam," I began, still facing forward.

He turned.

Three, two, one, GO!

I gulped and said, "So are you going to the, um, the... uh..." My voice suddenly stalled out like a Cessna mid-flight.

He furrowed his brow. "Are you okay?" he asked.

"Oh, I'm great," I said quickly. "How are you?"

"Good."

"Cool!"

"So what were you saying?"

Are you going to the dance next Friday, Adam Worley? Or wait. No. It's THIS Friday now. Does that mean I have to amend the question? Should I mention Friday at all? I don't know, I don't know, I don't know...

"I, um, I was just wondering if you—"

And right then, like a thunderclap, the stupid bell rang. I jumped so hard I practically fell out of my seat. Adam's hand shot out to catch me and I turned the color of a pomegranate.

"I'm good!" I said a little too loudly. A few people looked.

"Um," Adam began to say, but was cut off as Mr. Bowen bounded to the front of the room, booming about how we had a big day ahead. Today we were going to learn about *time travel.*

"Or at least, sort of," he clarified. "It's really more of a lesson about energy and light speed, but still. It's cool."

So with that, he launched into something to do with Einstein, which ordinarily I would've found fascinating except now all I was thinking was: *I'd give anything for an actual time machine right now...*

And thus began the sitting and waiting. Minute after minute passed as we all time traveled into the future at a snail's pace. Mr. Bowen lectured. People asked questions. Diagrams got drawn on chalkboards.

I didn't hear any of it. I was locked in my own private little world of heart-thumping misery. My eyes were glued to the clock. I couldn't decide if I wanted it to speed up or stop altogether.

Then—out of nowhere—an unexpected opportunity.

"Okay, I want you all to flip to page one thirty-six," Mr. Bowen said. "Work with your lab partners to answer questions one through four. They're about "Work and Energy." Pay attention to how they relate to what I was just saying about relativity."

Okay, *now* was the time. The room would be loud, filled with commotion. I had several minutes to do it. I could just slip it into the conversation. He'd ask something about question number three, and I'd say something like, *"yeah, energy is neither created nor destroyed, and speaking of which, do you want to go to the dance with me on Friday?"*

Easy.

I could do this.

The class was still quiet as everyone got their books out. A low rustling of zippers and Velcro. Adam leaned over to his bag and then sat up, empty-handed.

"Crap," he muttered. He looked over at me and whispered, "I think I forgot my book at home."

And then *this* happened:

"Adam Worley," I stated loudly. "There is a Sadies Dance this Friday, January the fifteenth, and I'd like to go to it with you. Would you like to go to it with me?"

This was one of those moments where the whole world stands still because what you just said was so unbelievably awkward that no one—including the surrounding wildlife—knows what to do. It was *that* bad.

The silence literally blanketed the room like a fog. I froze. For a moment, I wondered if I had truly said it out loud or not. It was possible I hadn't…

Then, with the slow inevitability of an avalanche, the laughter started. The whole class burst into a fit of hysterics, and there I was, sitting in the middle of it, red as a turnip.

Meanwhile, Adam just knitted his brow and stared at me, perplexed. After what seemed an eternity, I did the only thing I knew how to do: I carefully scooted my chair back, stood, and with great consideration, started to crawl under the desk.

I was halfway there when Adam exclaimed, "Whoa, wait!"

I stopped mid crouch. The classroom hushed. I looked at him.

"Definitely," he said.

"Definitely?" I repeated.

He smiled sheepishly. "I mean… yeah." He paused, blushing. (We were basically speaking in front of an audience now) "I was actually planning on asking *you,*" he confessed. "I was just waiting till after class. Sorry?"

My mouth moved but no words came out. *He* was going to ask *me?* What about the whole "Sadie Hawkins" thing? What about all the pressure from Sid? What about my deadline? What if I'd waited like *ten more minutes?*

"Well," I squeaked. "I mean…that's, um, well… *crap!*"

The class erupted in laughter again. I felt my cheeks about to burst. With as much dignity as I could muster, I scooted my chair back into place and sat regally with my hands folded. Adam looked at me, his deep brown eyes searching. I refused to meet them. My heart had suddenly paused, stuck in place. It was like it was asking, "*Shall I keep going, old girl? Or shall I call it quits?*"

Then, from the corner of my eye, I saw Adam's face light up. He was smiling—a bright, genuine smile that pulled me to him like a magnet. And just like that, my blush turned into something else entirely.

"Yes," I said loudly, now facing him. "Keep going please."

He tilted his head, obviously having no idea what I was talking about.

But my heart did.

And it did.

THREE DAYS

DRESS SHOPPING. This was *not* something I ever thought I'd be doing. And from the look on Thu's face as we entered the store, it wasn't something she thought she'd ever be doing either.

My *mother*—on the other hand—was very pleased. Despite her outward appearance of being an Olympic athlete (pole vaulter, maybe?), she still nurtured an inner fondness for "girly" things. Plus, she was all too aware of the fact that this was my very first high school dance. Technically, a boy named Tommy Elbert had asked me to Homecoming freshman year, but then he stood me up and my parents took me to Burger King instead. After that, my friends and I made a pact that dances were inherently lame and should be boycotted at all cost. Now, however, we all had dates, so…

Anyway, I was actually really glad Mom was with us. I didn't have a clue where to begin. I owned precisely *one* dress, which had been a gift from my aunt two Christmases ago. I'd worn it precisely once—and that instance happened to coincide with us visiting her in Orlando last year.

"So." Mom clapped her hands. "What do you girls think?"

Thu and I both stared at the endless wall of dresses before us. It was like a collage of Disney movies, overlapping in shiny reds and blues and purples and yellows. Some were sleek, others were ruffled; others were sleek *and* ruffled. Which was appropriate? Which would match my skin tone? Which would I look pretty in? Which would Adam like? Which would be, like, *comfortable?*

"Um," I finally answered. "That one?"

Basically I was pointing at the one dress in the whole store that was probably a Halloween costume. It looked like something straight out of *Cinderella* with a giant, poofy princess skirt and an explosion of ruffles at the shoulders. It was also bright orange.

"Well," Mom said hesitantly. "I mean, we don't have to decide right away. Tell you what, let's just start grabbing dresses and trying them on. How does that sound?"

Thu and I both shrugged in unison. "Okay," we said.

With that, we retreated to the changing rooms while Mom brought us a continuous stream of dresses like a human conveyor belt. "Oh, try *this* one!" she kept saying each time. Thu and I both giggled hysterically as we modeled them for each other, both feeling uniquely absurd.

"I wonder what would happen if I showed up in sweat-pants," Thu mused, frowning at her latest dress. "You think Joshua would get mad?"

I raised an eyebrow at her. "Ah, so it's *Joshua* now?"

She looked up, blushing. "Well. Yeah. I'm not going to call the boy I'm kissing 'Dawson's Creek.'"

I suddenly imagined Thu and Dawson's Creek cuddling together on a park bench and her whispering, 'I love you too, Dawson's Creek,' and I quickly agreed with her. "I guess that would be weird," I said with a little snort. Then I added delicately, "So... what *happened* with you guys? How come it didn't work out that night at the restaurant?"

She took a long breath and looked at me. "It's... compli-cated," she said.

I waited expectantly until finally she said, "I don't know. It was like that Zombie play you guys did. Like how the main zombie—Jessica Alvarez *sucked,* by the way—kept trying to grab them, but kept missing? That's what it was like with me and him. When he was mad, I was trying to reach out to him.

And when I was mad, that's when he was trying to reach out to me. It's like we just kept… missing."

I nodded. Just hearing the word "zombie" gave me a sudden pit in my stomach. It reminded me of that horrible month I spent lying in bed, and how I'd missed out on the whole play. I'd been so mad, and yet so *energyless* at the same time. I never wanted to feel that way again. Although to be honest, I was feeling pretty "energyless" right now, trying on all these silly dresses. I didn't look right in *any* of them. I just wanted to close my eyes, point at one, and be done with it. Then, after that, close my eyes for real and lie down for a while. I could've fallen asleep in an instant. But there was *no way* I was admitting that out loud. Everyone would go crazy (and by "everyone," I mean Mom), and I'd get rushed off to a hospital or something.

Totally unnecessary. And *not* going to happen. I was going to this dance no matter what. I'd already missed the school play; I wasn't going to miss dancing with Adam Worley too. Besides, who wouldn't get tired shopping all day? Especially if they felt like a complete fish out of water the whole time.

So yeah. That's all it was. I was fine.

When I looked up, though, Thu was already staring at me. "Are you okay?" she asked.

I smiled weakly. "Fine," I said. Then I gestured to the dress I was currently wearing. "I think I kinda like this one," I said, smoothing the ruffled fabric. "What do you think?"

She knitted her brow. My current dress was probably the ugliest one I'd tried on all day—a deep brown color with embroidered fabric and way too many ruffles. Why had Mom even brought this one, anyway?

"It's, um… nice?" she offered.

"I think so too," I said confidently. I turned to look in the mirror again and twisted to get a full body view. Definitely an ugly dress. I looked like a walking hotdog with wings.

"This is the one," I said with a nod, then called, "Mom!"

She appeared in an instant. "Find one you like?" she asked hopefully.

"What do you think of this one?" I said, half turning.

She made the exact same face as Thu. "Um… well I just wanted to experiment with the brown on your skin tone, but… do *you* like it?"

I nodded enthusiastically, feeling a sudden wave of dizziness. I quickly put a hand on the mirror to steady myself. "It's great," I lied.

Mom's voice changed. "Sweetie, are you all right?" she asked, stepping closer.

I smiled again. "Why does everyone keep asking that? I'm fine. Really. Should we just take this dress to the counter then?"

Not listening, Mom put her hand to my forehead. "Chloe, you're burning up…"

"Duh." I rolled my eyes. "That's because it's an inferno in here." I looked to Thu for confirmation and attempted a laugh. "Right?"

She looked at me plaintively. "I mean, yeah," she said, angling her voice toward my mom. "It is pretty hot in here, Mrs. Cartwright. Maybe we should take a break?"

Mom continued to study my face. "Chloe, you need to be honest with me, okay? How do you feel right now?"

"I'm fine," I insisted.

"Do you want to sit down?" she asked, and then nodded, as if answering her own question. "Come on," she said softly. "Let's go out to the front and rest for a minute."

"I'm really okay," I said again, but I let her lead me by the arm anyway.

Thu followed us to a bench in the main showroom. Mom sat next to me, stroking my hair and staring so intently at my face it was like she was trying to memorize every single skin cell.

"Mom, I'm fine," I repeated. I really just wanted to make her feel better. She looked so worried, I didn't know what else to say.

"Honey," she said, and then stopped herself.

I looked at her.

After a second, she tried again. "Do you... actually *want* that dress?"

It seemed like such an odd thing to say, given how scared she looked. I blinked at her and saw her eyes—halfway between laughing and crying.

"It's pretty ugly, huh?" I said with a wince.

"It is," she agreed. "Let's go home, okay? We can always pick out a dress tomorrow. There's still plenty of time."

I gave her a serious look. "Mom, I *need* to go to this dance, understand? I can't miss it."

"I know," she said quietly. "You won't miss it. I promise."

I stared at her a moment longer, silently asking, *Do I have your word on that?*

She nodded, saying, "Let's just get you home," and started to stand. She and Thu both gripped my arms, helping me up. I put my weight on my feet and realized I weighed a solid ton.

"Sorry," I said.

Yet as soon as I was upright, I knew what was coming. I'd felt it a dozen times before. It was always the same—no warning whatsoever.

I'm not sure if you've ever fainted before, but it's a pretty unique experience. You feel tingly for a split second and the next thing you know, you wake up somewhere else. It's like being teleported through time. One second you're in a dress shop, the next second you're in...

TWO DAYS

…A HOSPITAL WITH DR. MARK standing high above you. He was studying my chart so intently, he didn't notice my eyes open. Without moving my head, I looked around the room. Everything seemed blurry like I was looking up from warped glass. Even the beeps and hospital noises seemed to blend together in a muted haze. I didn't recognize the room. It must have been a new one.

After a moment, an extremely deep voice said, "There you are," and I blinked upward, focusing.

"Hi, Dr. Mark," I whispered. My voice was so frail, I could barely hear it. It was all thin and raspy, like I'd been yelling all night at a concert. "Where's my mom?"

"She's just outside," he said, indicating with a nod. "Your father's here too. I'll go get them."

I tried to put a hand out to stop him, but nothing happened. I was so weak I could barely move my fingers. He noticed and stopped.

"Dr. Mark," I whispered hoarsely. He leaned closer. "Just tell me," I said. "What's happening?"

He stood back up, found a stool and wheeled it over. Sitting down, he said, "Do you remember what happened yesterday?"

I thought a moment. "Dresses?" I answered weakly. I felt like I was going to drift back into sleep at any moment and had to fight to stay awake. I blinked up at him and he nodded. "That's right," he said. "You were with your mom at the dress shop when you fainted. An ambulance came and brought you to the emergency room. You—" He stopped and his face suddenly tightened. His eyes dropped for a moment until he looked back up. "You were touch and go for a while, Chloe," he said softly. "The important thing is that you're stable now and you're in the ICU. Do you understand?"

My brain was swimming. The world kept getting murkier and it was hard to concentrate. I refocused on Dr. Mark's face. It looked so much sadder than I'd ever seen before. I swallowed to find my voice. "Am I better?" I asked.

His eyes smiled as he cupped a giant hand on my forehead. "Of course," he said. "We're quite good at what we do, you know."

I attempted to smile back at him, but it was too hard. Everything was fading. "What about my…" my voice trailed off.

His hand moved to mine, gripping it gently. "Chloe, listen to me," he said.

My eyes blinked back open.

"I need you to be brave, okay? I need you to *fight*. Can you do that for me?"

I nodded smally. But even as I tried, the world kept getting fuzzier. Dr. Mark was barely more than a dark blur hovering over me. I wanted to say something—to finish a thought. I whispered it, yet nothing came out. No more strength to my voice. Dr. Mark bent forward. "Chloe?" he asked, his voice blurring along with the rest of him.

I blinked and my eyes stayed closed. I was fully underwater now. Sleep was pulling me deeper. It was dark and warm and all I wanted was to keep sinking—down, down, down.

But then, with an odd clarity, I heard my own voice utter a final word before letting go.

It said, "dance."

• • •

When I woke up I was still too weak to move. My voice was brittle and it was hard to breathe.

Nurses and Dr. Mark flowed in and out, while my parents sat immovable beside me like a pair of smooth stones in a stream. Both had tearstains on their cheeks that never seemed to leave. I tried my best to talk to them, to tell them I felt okay, but it was hard to form the words. I kept pausing in the middle of sentences, trying to catch my breath. They both told me to save my strength. No need to say anything. Just rest.

So a month ago, when I started feeling so much better, I kind of lied to you again. It's not that I didn't feel better, that part was true. I felt *a lot* better. It's just that I left something out. Dr. Mark had explained it. I was experiencing an immune system rebound, which was a good thing—just not a *permanent* good thing. No one, he'd explained, could fully predict *when* the end would come, only that it *would* come. The worst part was the airplane analogy. I could tell that he'd hated every second of telling it to me, but he had to do it. It went like this: When an airplane starts losing fuel and it's going to crash, it has an emergency reserve. This gets it to safety, if safety is nearby. The human body has the same thing. It throws its last reserves at the problem in one final effort to get to safety. But when it can't get there in time... there's nothing left.

So that was yesterday. The reserve tanks had finally run out. Now it was just a matter of gravity.

The day passed with me drifting in and out of sleep. Sometimes I'd wake up and feel slightly better, other times I'd wake up and feel much worse. Either way, my parents never left. They were always there every time I opened my eyes. By nighttime, I noticed that they were both taking turns at my side, brushing soft, trembling fingers across my cheeks. I wondered why, until I figured it out. There were tearstains on mine, too.

• • •

This next part, I'm almost positive, was a dream. I woke up in the dead of night to find my parents fast asleep in the chairs next to my bed. The hospital was quiet, with only the occasional nurse drifting by. Soft beeps. Hushed voices. And for some reason, I had an inexplicable urge to escape. I needed fresh air. I needed to be *away*.

So with great care, I slowly sat up and gently swung my legs off the bed. (I definitely couldn't have moved like that earlier in the day, so... dream.) Yet, dream or no, I cautiously tiptoed out of the ICU and made my way toward the elevators. I stayed close to the walls, sneaking along like a spy. When I reached my objective, I tapped the "up" button repeatedly until the doors opened. I slipped inside and pressed the top floor.

The next thing I knew, the elevator opened onto a long empty corridor. At the end of it was a service door, clearly labeled "Emergency Exit Only." I glided toward it and pushed it open. Now I was on the hospital's roof, overlooking the dark, empty streets below. For a second, I wondered what the heck I was doing up here. Why I had pressed "up," instead of "down?" Not a very wise escape plan.

Then a powerful snort came from behind me and I knew instantly. I turned and saw Hank, looking back at me with his giant red eyes. He truly was a terrifying creature—absolutely nothing *Disney* about him. Yet he didn't scare me in the slightest.

"Hello," I said, and reached out a hand.

He snorted again and bent down to let me pet him. His scales were smooth and hard as stones. The horns that rimmed his cheekbones were sharp too, like spikes. Yet he was very gentle with his movements. He didn't want to hurt me. Quite the opposite, in fact.

"I guess I'm dreaming," I said with a small smile.

He tilted his massive head, but gave no response. I ran my hand over his nose again.

"Thanks for earlier," I told him, bringing up another hand. "For giving me those extra weeks."

His head gave a slight bob.

I smiled again, but this time with a little conspiracy. "I don't suppose... you can give me a few more?"

I watched him hopefully. He snorted. But no head bob.

"Had to ask," I said.

I then turned and sat on the edge of the roof, looking out over the peaceful streets below. All empty—glowing yellow under the streetlamps. Hank's giant head came to rest beside me. I put a hand on him.

And that was it. We just sat there, watching the dark. No zombies this time. No walls of flame. Just a quiet, quiet night.

ONE DAY

BUT HANK *DID* GIVE ME another miracle. When I woke up, I felt better than the day before. Not *better*, better—just… better. My voice had crawled back. I could move without hurting. Breathing was easier.

I still couldn't walk, but I was strong enough to sit up. And for the very first time the room was empty, save for all the beeping machines. I also noticed that I'd apparently slept all day. It was late afternoon judging by the waning light from the window. Mom and Dad were probably getting something to eat. Besides, they still had Henry to take care of. I wondered where he was. I hoped they knew I needed to see him one last time.

There was a quick knock on the door and—expecting my parents—I turned.

But… not parents. Not Henry. Not even Dr. Mark.

It was Tad Prescott. And Miss Collins?

"Um, hi," I said, trying to sit up a little more. I felt suddenly embarrassed in my current state. Hospital gowns and IV tubes were hardly a flattering look.

Miss Collins shot forward, putting out a hand. "No, no, don't trouble yourself, please. We're here for your escape."

I tilted my head. *Escape?*

I wondered if I was still dreaming. My waking hours and sleeping ones were blending together more and more these days. Still, it didn't *feel* like a dream. Everything seemed way too real.

I lay back, knitting my brow a little. "Escape?" I asked.

Tad moved into the room after double-checking the hallway. "Operation Rolling Thunder," he said quickly, as if it were completely obvious what that meant. "We're just waiting for your doctor."

"Operation what?"

"Rolling Thunder. I'll give you a guess who came up with the name. How are you feeling?"

I grinned, looking between the two of them. I should've known.

Sid.

It dawned on me that it was actually pretty weird he hadn't visited yet. Clearly, he was up to something.

"I'm okay," I said, though my voice was still softer than I would've liked. "And I'm guessing Sid put you up to this?"

Tad nodded and Miss Collins smiled down at me. "You're looking a bit livelier today," she said. "We popped by yesterday, but you were snoozing."

"Been doing a lot of that lately," I said.

"So where is this doctor of yours?" she asked, glancing over her shoulder. "We're losing daylight."

"Daylight?"

She looked back down and grinned. "You'll see," she said.

Right then, Dr. Mark swept into the room with his usual flare. "All right," he said, still staring down at a chart. "I'm here for Operation Rolli—" he looked up, noticing Tad and Miss Collins. "Oh," he said abruptly. "Sorry." He stepped forward, extending a hand. "You must be Chloe's teacher."

Miss Collins took it. "Poppy," she said.

"Poppy," he repeated, sounding a little mulish with his deep American accent. "I'm Mark." There was an odd silence as they kept holding each other's hands staring at each other.

"Um," Dr. Mark said, suddenly flustered. "I just, uh… I just pictured someone different. Older," he said.

She smiled. "And I wasn't expecting a *giant*. Are you literally seven feet tall?"

Now even more mulish, he answered, "Uh... almost?"

"Hit your head on lots of doorways then?"

"I do."

Oh, and by the way, they were *still* holding hands.

And no, the significance of this was *not* lost on me.

Then, as if being jolted awake, they let go of each other and looked at me. "Chloe." Dr. Mark grabbed his stool and slid it over. "I need you to be really honest with me now, okay?"

I blinked up at him. "I'll do my best."

"I need you to tell me how you're feeling. You're vitals are looking great and I've just looked over your latest labs. But I need to hear it from you too. Are you feeling better?"

I shifted. He seemed so earnest, it made me a little nervous. "I mean... I feel better than yesterday," I said. "And I can, like, *sit up*, and stuff. Why? What's going on?"

He looked me over a moment, frowning. Then, as if deciding something, he nodded and asked, "You down for a little field trip?"

"A field trip?"

"It's not far," he said. "But it will get you out of this room. Do you think you're up for it?"

For some reason, Dr. Mark, Miss Collins and Tad were all being extremely cagey about exactly *what* was going on. It felt like I was being set up for a surprise party or something. In fact, *was* it a surprise party? That would've been really nice, but I wasn't exactly feeling up for a party. Still, the thought of going anywhere that wasn't here sounded like heaven on Earth. I definitely didn't want to end my days in this beeping hospital room. So with that, I said, "Definitely," and grinned as broadly as I could.

Dr. Mark grinned back. "That's my girl. Now get ready for a little adventure. I'm about to break every bureaucratic rule this hospital has to offer, but I'm confident it will all work out. After all, I'm kind of a big deal around here. You ready?"

As if he had to ask. The beeps from my heart monitor dramatically picked up the pace as I nodded excitedly.

"Good," he said. He turned to Tad. "You're on elevator duty. I want you to run ahead and keep the doors open, understand?"

Tad nodded. "On it," he said, and ducked out of the room.

Dr. Mark turned back to me. "All right, your teacher and I are going to wheel you out of here. Everything you need is attached to the bed, so don't worry about a thing. I'll be with you the whole time."

I gave him a weak thumbs up and settled back into the pillows. Wherever we were going, I felt safe knowing he'd be there.

It took him a second to double-check all the monitors and tubes and then we were rolling. He led the bed from the front while Miss Collins pushed from the back. The surrounding hospital drifted past us. An occasional nurse would glance in our direction but most of them were too busy to pay much attention. Before I knew it, we were at the elevators, gliding in as Tad held the doors.

"Ground floor." Dr. Mark pointed.

"Oh, right," Tad said, jumping forward and pushing the button.

On the ride down (hospital elevators are notoriously slow) there was a palpable tension. Not a bad one, though. The opposite. It was that awesome nervousness you get when you're about to jump out of an airplane, or, you know, ask someone to a dance. (Not a random example, of course.)

Once the doors opened we made our way through the corridors until we reached a pair of giant sliding doors. I quickly recognized that we were moving into the hospital's outdoor courtyard. I'd only walked through it once before when I was healthier. It was huge—almost the size of a public park. There were tables, benches, long stretches of grass, and even a little stream with imported fish.

Also—of much greater consequence—it was currently *packed*. People were everywhere, sitting, standing, munching on snacks, and when they noticed us, quickly parted like a giant curtain. At first, I just thought they were regular visitors—people I didn't know. A lot of them were adults and kids that I didn't recognize. After a moment though, I started seeing more and more familiar faces. Students from my school. Teachers. Neighbors. Family friends. They all beamed as I rolled through. I searched for Sid or Thu or Dawson's Creek, but they weren't there. *What are they up to?* I wondered. *They must be here somewhere...*

Then, very suddenly and very loudly, a strange whistle pierced the air. It sounded vaguely familiar, like maybe I'd heard it in a movie once. I kept trying to place it until I heard a new sound. Water. Or better yet, *seawater* breaking against the sides of an old sailing ship. Gentle rocking and creaking wood. A slight breeze. Flapping canvas.

Pirates of the Caribbean?

Pirates of the Caribbean!

A hush had fallen over the crowd and all the faces began to duck out of sight. I sat up to see. For a second, I just blinked in astonishment. There were chairs everywhere—foldout chairs, lined up in neat rows, one after the other, in long rectangles. There were at least a hundred. Looking forward, I realized I was being wheeled through an empty lane, kind of like the isle between pews at a wedding.

And there, now visible in front of me was a... *something?* A stage? It looked like a big, boxy platform. A giant curtain fell behind it, hanging on tall poles. And if it *was* a stage, it was completely empty. The ocean sounds were coming from a pair of speakers on either side.

I knitted my brow in confusion. Everyone seemed to know what was going on except me. Dr. Mark and Miss Collins quietly angled my bed into an upright position and locked the wheels in place. I was right in the center of the audience, not too close and not too far away. Best seat in the house.

A total silence blanketed the courtyard. There was only the gentle lapping of small waves against the ship. Minutes passed as everyone settled in and the anticipation rose. I—for one—couldn't wait to see what Sid had cooked up. In fact, I was *already* enjoying myself. It was one of those perfect afternoons with a pink sun and a gentle breeze rustling the surrounding trees. Dr. Mark had brought extra blankets and put two of them on me. I looked up at him for any clues, but he just shrugged his massive shoulders and looked ahead.

And—as I've mentioned—Dr. Mark is an insanely tall human being. So when I looked up, I also caught a glimpse of the hospital's roof. I wasn't surprised at all. Hank was there, perched right on the edge. I guess he was just as curious as me.

I stared a moment longer until my attention was drawn back to the stage. A lone figure appeared from behind the curtain.

He was a pirate.

Well, he was Sid. But he was dressed like a pirate. Big black hat. Cutlass. Pointy goatee. Captain's jacket. Eye patch.

He strode onto the middle of the stage and stood there a moment in silence. He eyed the audience with menace, crossing his arms and squinting through his good eye. Then, very suddenly, he relaxed and wore an easy smile.

"I'm actually not a pirate," he said casually, using his normal voice. It seemed incredibly out of place, given the costume. I was expecting a lot of *"arghs!"* and *"ahoy mateys!"* but instead it was just regular Sid.

"The truth is," he continued. "I'm an officer with Starfleet."

A light chuckle rippled through the audience. I grinned, shaking my head.

"My name is Captain Siddhartha Patel of the *U.S.S. Timeless,*" he said loudly, putting on an air of authority. "I was sent here on a very important mission that until now I've had to keep secret. I apologize for the deception, of course, but it was necessary. You see, when it comes to time travel, there isn't any room for error. No one could suspect that I, or my crew, were actually from the future.

"Now you may be wondering, 'if the future, Captain Patel, why the pirate outfit?' Well, it is my hope that over the next hour, that question will be answered in detail. For the moment, however, I wish to say a few words about the reason all of us are here. It is why you are listening, and why I traveled through time.

"Sixteen years ago, a seminal moment in the history of humankind occurred in the very building that stands behind you. Sean Cartwright and his far too beautiful wife, Patricia, had a daughter. They named her Chloe. What neither of them knew at the time—and of course, how could they?—was that this little girl would go on to save the universe." He nodded briskly. "Not just a piece of it, mind you. The *entire thing.*" He then raised his voice even louder. "Which brings us to the mandate of the *U.S.S. Timeless.* It is a very different sort of ship from most Starfleet vessels. It travels solely through time, not space. It explores the past. It visits the present. It protects the future. And its latest mission brings it here, today, to provide you a glimpse of the most remarkable human being I have ever known. Today we take a look at the life of Chloe Cartwright, a young woman who I am most fortunate to call my best friend. She has changed my life. She has touched all of yours. And soon, as you will discover, she will rescue us all.

"This story begins on the nineteenth day of your November, stardate 304116.58. I ask you now to lend me your ears. Let me show you the person I know so well. Let me show you who she was, who she is, and indeed, who she will become. For Chloe Cartwright's story is only just beginning. Her destiny lies up there!" He suddenly threw his hand skyward, stepping backward. "Amongst the stars! Her continuing mission: To explore strange new worlds! To seek out new life and new civilization! To boldly go where no one has gone before!"

With that, he took his final step back, disappearing through the curtain. The audience cheered and I... well, I *tried* to clap. Mostly I just wiped tears from my eyes so I could see. I felt Dr. Mark put a hand on my shoulder. "You okay?" he asked quietly, his deep voice cutting through the applause.

I nodded, sniffling.

A moment later the cheering quieted and the play began.

Everyone was in it. Sid, Thu, Dawson's Creek, Tad, Jen, Piya, Mom and Dad (plus Henry), Emily Sulecki, ADAM WORLEY, Mr. Bowen, Miss Collins, the Mathletes, the Chess Club, Speech and Debate, my entire Drama class—everyone had a role.

A play like this wasn't something that got thrown together in a day or two. It had props, costumes, sound effects, set pieces, a *script...*

Sid had been working on this a long time. Months. At least. I felt a sudden wave of foolishness. All this time I'd thought my "Plan" had been the only one. Yet all the while, my friends had been working on a plan of their own. Secret meetings. Secret rehearsals. And that one horrible month when no one visited—*this* is what they'd been up to. What had Tad called it? Operation Rolling Thunder?

I shook my head.

That *was* a better name than "The Plan." It was also very Sid-like.

There was this one time when we were all playing Dungeons & Dragons at Thu's house last summer. Her dad had walked through and asked us, "Aren't you guys a little old for this?" I mean, he kind of had a point, right? A bunch of teenagers playing D&D? I don't know if you've ever witnessed a campaign or not, but it *is* pretty dorky. It's all spells, wizards, basilisks and Bags of Holding.

At the time, Thu simply shooed him away and we kept playing. None of us—at least that I know of—thought anything of it. We'd simply been playing the game since we were kids and didn't see any reason to stop. But here's the thing, and there's really no way around this: You're never too old for imagination. It doesn't matter if you're fifteen or a hundred and fifteen, imagining a better world is what it's all about. It's the picturing of what *could be*—what *should be*— that makes us human. It's hope.

And hope, my dear reader, is what Sid was giving to me now. This performance was more than a play. It was more than actors on a stage. It was more than a farewell.

It was showing me what *could be*.

Perhaps I wasn't going to die today. Or tomorrow. Perhaps my destiny lay, like Sid said, up *there*. In the stars. Strange new worlds. New civilization. It was waiting for me, ready to be explored.

Chloe Cartwright—played by Thu Pham—joined Starfleet on this day, leaving the 21st century behind. She traveled to the past, where indeed she *did* become an Expert in Pirate Affairs and Professional Treasure Hunter. She traveled to the future, where she captained a ship, naming it *Serenity* in honor of a previous life. During her travels, she met the great, great, great, great grandson of Adam Worley, who by some miracle looked *exactly* like his forbearer. They had a dalliance. And then, in the end, she traveled alone to the edge of known space, where she saved the universe. How did she do it exactly? Well... I'll let you use your imagination.

During the final scene, Sid reappeared in his pirate costume. He smiled, as everyone now knew precisely why he was wearing it. Always best to end a story where it began—a lesson we'd all learned from Dungeons & Dragons. As he spoke, I noticed a great gust of wind from above. A beating of giant wings.

I looked up and saw Hank flying away. He'd left his perch for the open air, letting out a final screech that echoed across an orange sky. I knew in that moment I'd never see him again. I didn't need to. He'd done his job; now he was off to help someone else. I—Chloe Cartwright—had a universe to save.

"And so that is how it began," Sid announced, removing his cap into a sweeping bow. "She was born right here. This very spot. It shall be marked in the annals of history forevermore. That much, I assure you. After all, I am the captain of the *U.S.S. Timeless.* I know a thing or two about history.

"Chloe, ladies and gentlemen! We owe this night to her. We love her. We treasure her. She is why we are here."

He stopped and looked directly at me, his chin slightly quivering. "Chloe," he said. "I love you so much. Thank you for being my best friend."

My throat tightened and he bowed again, staying low.

All was silent. No one dared to breathe.

Then, when he rose, the world rose with him. The audience erupted in applause, shooting to their feet. The other players filed out from behind the curtain. Mom and Dad. Thu and Dawson's Creek. They all linked hands. Bowed. The ovation grew louder, thunderous. I had too many tears to see. I clapped and laughed and wiped my eyes and clapped some more. In that moment, I didn't feel weak at all. A surge of joyous strength flowed through me. I cried and cried.

The applause grew louder. There was laughter. I felt a hand on me. Then another and another. I pried my eyes open through a wall of tears. Tried to focus. Beaming faces all around.

I figured it out eventually. All that applause and all those shouts—and no one was facing the stage.

It wasn't the play they were cheering for.

It was me.

ZERO DAYS

THAT NIGHT, I passed away.

It happened some time around three or four. I couldn't really be sure. I kept drifting in and out of sleep. It was peaceful, though. I know that much. It just kind of came, like it was no big deal. I drifted off, falling asleep, then drifted a little further.

And that, as they say, was that.

Sid was there. Mom and Dad. Henry. Everyone in the play. They all crowded into the small room, none of them willing to leave. I remember tears. I remember smiles. I remember Sid telling me some weird joke about a chicken and a duck. But do you know what I remember most? I remember all of their presence.

There's this great line in *Firefly* (I know, right? *Again* she mentions this show), where Captain Malcolm Reynolds says, as the ship is running out of air and he chooses to stay behind, "Everyone dies alone."

Well, Mal, this time I've got ya. You were finally wrong about something.

I didn't die alone.

I died surrounded by those I love most. I was as un-alone as a person can get.

?

OH, RIGHT. Henry's letter.

I figure I might as well share it with you. After all, I mentioned it several times and you're probably curious. It's meant for him, of course, but I made my parents promise to hold onto it until he's old enough to read it. That'll be like, *at least,* a decade away. Way too long to wait. Besides, where I am now, there is much to be done. I can't really describe any of it with *words,* per se, or, for that matter, where I am. What I can tell you is this: It sure ain't what anyone has ever imagined, and no one—even if he or she is mean—has anything to be afraid of. That's the most important part.

Anyway. Henry's letter.

Here goes:

Dear Baby Bro,

You probably don't remember me, and that really sucks. I wish I could've gotten to know you better, and I super wish I could've seen you grow up. You had a cool look about you, even as a baby, and it would've been nice to discover I was right about that.

I'm not sure how most big sisters are, but I was looking forward to having a little brother. I wanted to hang out with you, gossip, give music advice, conspire against Mom and Dad, teach you how to talk to girls (there's quite an art to it), and yes, even argue about things.

Also, I would've been the way, way older-than-you big sister. I could've given you rides to parties, or picked you up at 3:00am when Mom and Dad would've freaked out. I could've bought you bottle rockets as a kid, and cheap booze when you got to college.

But as it turned out, life had different plans. So instead of me, you get this—a piece of paper. Kind of crappy, right? Not exactly an adequate substitute. But that's the way it works sometimes, kid. You get handed a bum deal and you have to make the most of it. That's what this letter is about. Since I won't be around to give you any advice later on, I'll have to cram it all in right here and now.

So. First lesson:

Be nice to Mom and Dad. They're cool, they deserve it, and they love you. Someday you'll think they're both really lame. This is inevitable. But just as inevitable is another day, a ways down the road, when you realize that they're not. They're people. They had lives of their own once. And no matter what, they will always be there for you. Remember that.

Eat your vegetables. But don't pretend to be one of those people who enjoys them. A cheeseburger will always taste better than a head of cauliflower. The point is to do what's right, even if it's unpleasant, because it's good for you, and because it's good for others. Be a man of character.

Shower regularly. Girls appreciate a boy who smells nice. There is no reason to deny them this.

Don't be a hater. Know that everybody out there is trying to do the best they can with what they've got. Sometimes people are jerks. Sometimes people are awesome. It's up to you, each and every day, to decide which one you want to be.

Exercise. Believe me when I tell you this one very, very true thing: Good health is everything. It's like the air you breathe. When it's there, you don't really think about it. When it's gone, you think of nothing else. So stay fit.

When it comes to school, pick something you like and stick with it. I guarantee you'll discover there's more to the world than meets the eye.

Try to love as many things as you can; try to be afraid of as few. Fear is one of the easiest emotions in existence, and it's also the most stupid. When you look at any problem in the world, you'll always find fear somewhere at its heart. My solution to this is really simple. If you're afraid of something, do it.

Obviously there are exceptions to this. If what scares you is hand-to-hand combat with a grizzly bear, then follow your gut and avoid that situation. But for most other things… don't be a wuss. Do it. Then, and only then, will you see there was nothing to be scared of in the first place.

Know that all good times end. Appreciate them while they last.

Know that all bad times end. Look forward to when the good ones return.

Don't worry about finding love. Be yourself, always. Some things can only be found when you're not looking.

Don't judge books by their covers. You never know what's going to surprise you, and sometimes the people you least expect will be the most extraordinary. Give them a chance.

Don't judge period. This isn't an easy thing to do, but try. Most of life is chance, and no one can ever truly know what it is to be in another's shoes. The best we can do is guess, and it's not enough.

Be nice. Sometimes a smile is all it takes.

Be tough. Sometimes a frown is all it takes.

Be there for your friends. You'll never regret it and they will always pay you back—many, many times over.

Watch Firefly. If you didn't like it, slap yourself upside the head, watch it again.

And here's a big one. I want you to remember this above all the others. When you find yourself in a tough spot, always, always, always remember to

Hmm.

Fudge nuggets.

Looks like I didn't get to finish. Writing letters is harder than it looks, you know. I must have figured I'd get back to it later. (Let that be a lesson to you...)

Anyway, I apologize for that. And if you happen to see Henry someday, maybe walking down the street, or perhaps pedaling a unicycle, tell him this from his big sister: "I'm sorry. I would've finished if I could, but time ran out. I guess the rest is up to you."

THE END

Want to know when the next book is coming out?
Sign up for C.W. Sims' email list. It's quick, it's easy
and he promises zero spam. Here's the link:
https://mailchi.mp/5448b04d4c71/subscribepage-colin-sims

Thank you for reading "Where the Dragons Go."

If you liked it, please take a second to leave a review. We authors thrive on reviews. They're super important for getting the word out.

Also, I write new adult sci-fi and fantasy books under my actual name, Colin Sims, so be sure to check them out. One is a humorous urban fantasy called, "True Magic," and the other is a sci-fi novel entitled, "Downfall."

Thanks again for reading.

About the Author

After growing up in the quiet suburbs of Silicon Valley, Colin Sims decided journalism might be a good way to see the world. Thus, after college, he moved to Cairo, Egypt where he studied Arabic and worked as a freelance reporter for three years. Once he returned to the U.S., he worked in television news but couldn't shake a growing desire to try his hand at fiction. So, in a fit of lunacy one day in 2011, Colin quit his job, bought a motorcycle, and spent the next few months riding across the country and writing his first manuscript. He has been dedicating himself to the craft ever since ...

You can find Colin on Facebook:
www.facebook.com/colinsimsauthor

Twitter: @colinsimswriter

Or reach him by email at: colinwsims@gmail.com